ALMOST DARK

ALMOST DARK

A NOVEL

LETITIA TRENT

OPEN ROAD
INTEGRATED MEDIA
NEW YORK

Copyright © 2016 Letitia Trent

Cover design by Mauricio Díaz

ISBN: 978-1-5040-6402-6

This edition published in 2020 by Open Road Integrated Media, Inc.
180 Maiden Lane
New York, NY 10038
www.openroadmedia.com

For my family in Vermont

ALMOST
DARK

The past is never dead. It's not even past.
—WILLIAM FAULKNER

I

I

―――――

SEPTEMBER 15TH, 1993

Claire and Sam went out to the factory that Friday night because they'd heard from Archie that high school kids went there to party on the weekends. According to Sam, Archie was a trusted source of illicit information: his father was a motorcycle mechanic, a job that Archie had somehow made seem exotic, and he let Archie drink beer and smoke in the house. Archie had only shrugged when Claire expressed shock that anyone's parents would let them smoke or drink.

"I guess we just do things differently," he'd said.

Sam insisted that Archie knew what was cool, and Claire knew enough to believe her brother. Archie knew that you called concerts *shows* instead of *concerts*. You called everything an album, even if it was a tape or a CD. He wore a Nine Inch Nails t-shirt—he'd gone to a concert, a *show*, in Albany, and Trent Reznor had spit on him. He told the story almost every time anyone mentioned going to a show or even listening to a new CD, and wore the shirt almost as often, though it had a small hole in one shoulder and was faded to a muddy grey instead of its original black. But the fading made it even better, and Archie somehow knew that, too. His hair was long and straight and he smoked cigarettes behind the school with another group of boys who bunched in a tight circle, mumbling short, cutting exchanges, sloping their shoulders inward and sliding quick, darting glances at anyone who passed. He smoked pot, too. He'd shown Claire and Sam a baggy full of something that looked like dried garden weeds and told them to inhale. Claire had stuck her nose in the bag and sneezed—it smelled like nothing she recognized.

"I stole it from my dad," he said, brushing his shaggy hair out of his eyes.

"If anyone finds out you have that," Claire said, "you could get kicked out." But she was too excited to be worried for him. She wanted her real life, her adult life, to begin and she had a feeling that Archie might be her way in.

Sam just laughed. "Nice," he said.

Their attention seemed to please Archie. He smiled and put the baggie in his back pocket.

"Can we have some?" Claire asked.

Archie laughed and punched her lightly on the shoulder. "You're too young, kid. Maybe in a couple of years."

Claire could feel that he liked to look at her. This was new. Usually, boys didn't notice her. She didn't quite know what to do with this new development, but she sensed it might benefit her. She wanted to be an adult. She'd recently thrown away her Barbies and bought her first real tube of lipstick, a reddish-brown color like Angela Chase wore on *My So-Called Life*.

"Oh, come on, Archie," she said. She met his eyes and held them for longer than usual. He looked away first.

"You don't know what you're asking, kid," He said. He sighed and put his hands in his pockets, world-weary, weighed down with so much forbidden knowledge. "It's really strong stuff," he told her, "almost like hash. Hash can really mess you up."

Claire knew hash only as a particularly disgusting meal of corned beef and potatoes, which her grandparents liked to eat with slices of buttered white bread. Her parents were not cool like Archie's dad—they went to the Methodist church every Sunday and her mom wouldn't let her watch *Blossom* because she'd heard on *Dateline* that the show had had a whole special about somebody losing their virginity. Claire had to get all of the good television—MTV, *Blossom*, *Life Goes On*, and *Tales From the Crypt*—at her friends' houses, where their parents were too busy working or arguing or doing whatever adults did all day to pay attention to what their kids were watching.

Sam told her later what hash was, after Archie had gone to shop class and nobody was around to make fun of her for not knowing.

"Hash is like pot," he explained, "only stronger. It makes you super high or something. It makes time slow down."

Time slowing down. The idea seemed terrifying to Claire. Why would anyone want time to be slower than it already was? Time was so slow that it seemed that ninth grade was taking months and months and months to finish.

Sam was Claire's twin. He was taller, better looking, smarter, and though they were the exact same age, he somehow seemed older. He looked like their mother, who had been called Snow White in high school (Claire had seen it scrawled in her old yearbook, under her impossibly pretty picture—her mother's eyes and lipstick and black hair against her clear, pale skin). Claire looked like her mother, too, but a smaller, mousier, less striking version.

It was as though Sam had sucked up all of the best genes in the womb and had left her with mediocrity.

The factory had almost burned down once, long before Claire and Sam had been born—long before they had even been imagined. Now, it was just a building that had always been there.

All the children of Farmington had to visit it in Elementary school—there was something special about the slate shingles, which had come from a nearby quarry, and its historical location. The children of Farmington were always having to look at some pieces of rock that supposedly had something to do with the state—marble slabs at the Capital building and quartzite rocks, halved and thick with crystals, at the mineral museum. Claire had seen every important rock in the state by the time she was out of elementary school. That's what came from living in a place where there was nothing much but rocks and maple syrup and snow.

Years ago, the factory had shut down for good. Somebody had gotten sick, sued for damages, and the place had been closed. Claire couldn't remember much about it. It had happened when she was a child. All she remembered were the news reports. That day, her parents had watched the local news intently. The news was finally going to mention Farmington. This never happened, except when Farmington was going to get a snowstorm that might knock down power lines and cause elderly people to freeze to death in their homes, and even then it was only a cloud-covered place on the weatherman's map, or a snow-choked road where a reporter stood in a blizzard, reporting about how dangerous it was to be outside. She had looked up from her crayons and soda and saw a place she knew on television—the Channel Six news trucks were right in front of the factory. Her mother had shooed her away from the television then, told her to get started on her homework, just as the real news was starting, and she never learned what had happened.

That Friday night, Claire begged Sam to take her to the factory. Their parents had gone to bed early, exhausted with stomach flu, which they'd had for the last week—and which Claire and Sam had mercifully avoided.

"You kids," their mother said, sounding almost angry. "You kids have the best immune systems. Never sick, and when you do get sick, you're always sick together."

And so they found themselves basically alone by nine p.m. on a Friday night.

"C'mon," Claire said. "It can't hurt to go. They'll never even know we were gone."

"I guess it can't hurt," Sam said, distracted. He'd been playing *The Legend of Zelda* while Claire watched. He could play video games for hours at a time, something that increasingly bothered her: it was one of the first interests they didn't share. She could see, already, that this would happen more and more as they got older. She didn't know if he had noticed this drift, if he cared. It was normal, after all, to separate from your siblings, from your family.

Sam held Claire's hand as they walked, navigating her around a piece of split sidewalk, the crack big enough to lodge a foot in. She would have tripped, maybe sprained or broken an ankle, if he hadn't guided her. Sam had good eyesight, or at least was better at seeing what was right in front of him. He was good at sports, too—a starter on the basketball team and one of the school's tennis stars. There was almost nothing that he wasn't good at. He wanted to be an attorney when he grew up, like the people on *L.A. Law*. Claire wanted to be a librarian because she liked to be around books. She remembered how the children's room librarians would sometimes pull big, colourful picture books from the shelves and read them out loud, slowly, lingering over the pictures.

"I used to love that," she'd told Sam, "how you could go to the library and sit down on those pillows and bean bag chairs and they would just read you a book out loud and you could just sit and imagine being somewhere else completely. It would be nice to do that for other kids, you know?"

Sam had not laughed when she told him her future hopes, though she knew he was probably a little bit disappointed—there had never been, and there never would be, a television show about librarians. Even L.A. librarians.

Claire was good at reading, at taking tests, at everything in school except for math, and even then she did reasonably well when tested. These gifts served her well in school, but she didn't know what they could do for her beyond that. Most people had talents in something real—fixing lawnmowers, drawing, writing, budgeting—not in test taking. She didn't do sports, not even field hockey, which everybody in town seemed to love. Even adults without children came to the high school hockey games. It had seeped mysteriously into the fabric of the town, so much so that her parents were surprised when she'd told them that she didn't want to play.

Claire hated falling on the ground and getting her hands and knees dirty, having to stand up with mud between her fingers, on her legs. She hated having to pretend to care if her ball went into the goal at the very end of the field. It was also hard for her to care when she thought of what would happen in the end: if they won, everybody went out for pizza; if they lost, everybody went out for pizza. She couldn't figure out why it mattered which event brought about the pizza at the end.

But worse, she dreaded the inevitable disappointment that her presence on a team seemed to inspire. Nobody said it out loud, but she could feel the general sigh and resignation from the other kids when she was assigned to their team during PE. And, because she was frightened of failing, whenever somebody passed her the ball she froze or swiped stiffly at it, knowing as soon as her stick met the ball that it would go in a direction that was of no help to anyone, or worse yet, the direction of somebody on the opposite team—someone who didn't care about the mud on her knees or squelching between her fingers, who wanted nothing more than to get the ball in the goal.

Instead of sports, Claire was a member of Quiz Bowl. She wasn't stupid—she knew it wasn't cool. But it was fun, and she didn't have the fear of letting her team down. She was good at remembering things heard in passing on television, or names and dates her eyes might have skimmed in a textbook or magazine. Her brain seemed to absorb everything equally—celebrity gossip and novel passages and quotes from films. She was the star of the team.

Being Sam's sister made it easier for her to be on the Quiz Bowl team instead of the hockey team. Even though she was shy and didn't know the right people, she knew that Sam would be there to bring the world to her. With Sam, she could do almost anything she wanted without being picked on or isolated. She was luckier than some of the other kids on the Quiz Bowl team, the ones who wore their pants too high, or had big plastic glasses and funny teeth or parents who spoke too loudly or clapped too long when they received the attendance award at the year-end assembly. They didn't have any buffer between themselves and the world at school, where real-life rules didn't yet apply. Someday, Kenny Walker, who had braces, thin, freckled arms, and had his books knocked out of his hands practically every time he stepped away from his locker, would probably live in the biggest house in Farmington because he could do complicated long division in his head and could put together things without looking at the diagrams. Or, more likely, he would leave Farmington altogether. But right now, he was miserable.

Sam protected her from their lonely lives. He protected her from having to live in imaginary worlds like Sheila, the Quiz Bowl science whiz, who obsessed over *Doctor Who* and could talk about almost nothing else. Claire liked to be around those kids during Quiz Bowl, where she could laugh at jokes about Pi, or about how the kids from Chesterville didn't know that Mark Twain's real name was Samuel Clemens. Afterward, though, she was happy to be with Sam again. He would make sure that she didn't drift off like Sheila, into a world that nobody else wanted to enter.

Claire squeezed Sam's hand and then dropped it as they made their way to the factory, to the newer, smoother strips of sidewalk. It was mid-September but still warm. Her mother called it an Indian summer; it was a strange, humid warmth with an edge of cold, just like early spring.

Her hands were both damp and cool. She wiped them on her jeans.

They walked past rows and rows of houses with the same design, same driveways and garages, same dingy paint. Most seemed empty, the windows dark and the porch lights off. But there were cars in some of the driveways. It was late, past eleven. She imagined the people inside, sleeping in their beds. Probably mostly older couples, judging by the absolute darkness in every window and the lack of toys or swing sets in their yards.

They went from streetlight to streetlight, walking more quickly when they passed through a stretch of darkness.

They reached the factory. Claire took Sam's hand. It was dark, far from the streetlights, set back away from the road. It was the last building in a row of former factories, some now converted into office buildings, others similarly abandoned. Beyond the factory, the roadside grew tangled and wild, the sidewalk ended, and only a few isolated houses remained tucked up away from the road, at the ends of long driveways.

"Come on," Sam said, dropping Claire's hand. He picked up his pace, his white tennis shoes flicking back and forth as he jogged away. The factory's grey slate walls were as familiar to Claire as any building in town—the high school, with its orange brick; the YMCA, with the scummy pool out back and the aqua-green tiling on the bathroom floors; or the post office, with the blue pens chained to the counter so they couldn't be stolen. She hesitated as Sam ran ahead. The windows were black and reflected nothing. There were no lights behind them, no rustles or voices or signs of movement.

At summer camp, when Claire was eleven—too old to admit to being scared but too young not to be—the camp counsellors had gathered the middle-school aged campers around the fire for ghost stories.

"Have you heard about the girl who haunts the old factory by the river?"

The girls all shook their heads.

The counsellor spoke with exaggerated honesty, in a tone that older girls used to fool younger girls, one that both acknowledged the lie and denied it. The girls knew she was making up a story to scare them, maybe because she was mean and wanted to make them cry or call their parents or pull their blankets in tight around their bodies. Still, they wanted to be told the story. They wanted to be afraid.

"Well," the counsellor said, sitting back so her face was out of the orange light of the fire, "the dead girl was just a little older than all of you." She pointed to Claire, to the girl seated next to her—another Quiz Bowl member who had braces and fat, white, dimpled knees—and then to the others in turn, her bangle bracelets jangling at her wrist.

"The murderer watched as the girl made her way back and forth, back and forth, every day from home to school." The counsellor shook her head slowly, back and forth, as if watching a slow tennis game. "He killed her on a day in late November, right before Thanksgiving break. She had stayed late at school for detention—chewing gum, nothing serious, she was a good kid. So she had to walk home on the empty street, the sky all cloudy, and she walked home in that almost dark—"

(Claire would remember that phrase, the *almost dark*. The phrase was tossed off, but for Claire it had summarized everything frightening about the factory. *In the almost dark* she'd sometimes think, even years later, when a shape in the corner assumed the form of a person and she'd have to close her eyes tight and shake her head before she could open them again and see only clothes draped on her dresser, her coat hanging from a hook.)

"—and that's how he got to her," the counsellor said, emphasizing the word *got* with a slap to her naked thigh, right below the hem of her khaki shorts.

"She was walking home alone, nobody on the road, no witnesses. She lived in one of those houses near the factory, past the sidewalk, way off in the woods. She was poor, like the people that live over there now, and she had to walk everywhere. He hit her on the head with a brick and buried her body in the parking lot of the factory. I hear her body's still there."

The story wasn't true, but it seemed so. Not the facts—how could a man bury somebody in the ground in a public place without anyone knowing?—but at least the spirit. At least that's how it seemed when Claire had returned from camp with her constellations of mosquito bites, her skin tanned, her shins bruised.

But Claire didn't trust her fears—Sam wasn't afraid, and he never had been. He said that it was just the colour of the factory, the colour of smoke or a lightning storm. It made it seem foreboding, like a castle in a movie. And the river was behind it, roaring and rock-choked. It was the kind of place you could fall in and crack your head and die and be swept away before anyone even knew you were gone. The factory was surrounded by gravel and pavement—no strips of grass, no decorative hedges to soften it and give it the impression of human intention or arrangement.

"It just *looks* spooky," Sam said. As though how a thing looks is different than what a thing is.

As they came upon the factory, as she began to hear the river's racket and smelled the damp rock, Claire told herself that it was just how empty it was, how dark it was, how she could hear the river, which had risen after late-summer rains and was swollen almost up to the banks.

"Come on!" Sam shouted again. He was far off—she could barely see him waving from the steps.

"Is anybody there?"

Sam stood on his tip-toes to see through the small window in the door. "I thought I heard some voices. Maybe Arch is here. Maybe we can finally get some weed from him."

Claire jogged forward to meet him.

Oh Jeez, she thought, what if Archie *was* there? She wished she'd brought her watermelon lip gloss, or even just her cherry ChapStick and a pocket comb.

"So, how do we get in?" she asked.

On the front steps, the darkness was deeper, and the streetlight hardly reached them—it only reflected in the windows, making them appear more opaque. Claire shivered when the wind kicked up from the river. As a child, she had never swum at the river's deepest points—it petered out farther west until it was only a shallow brook, a place to wade in the summer and let fish swim around your legs, sending a rash of goose bumps up your skin when their quick, strange bodies slid against your ankles. But children weren't allowed to play in the river here. The water was deep in the middle, taller than an adult, and people had died in it—mostly drunks stumbling around in the darkness, but sometimes healthy adults who had come to swim, sometimes children.

"Archie said there was an open window around here somewhere," Sam said. He jumped down from the steps. Claire heard the crunch of little pebbles beneath his shoes. "Come on."

Sam walked the perimeter of the building, touching each dark window, tapping the glass. They were now at the wall adjacent to the river. Claire couldn't see the river, but she could hear it and smell it—piles of wet rock, dry leaves, dirt, and salt.

"Look," Sam said. "This one's open." He bent over and passed his hand through the empty hole in the dark.

"I don't think I can fit through that," Claire said. The window was black and showed no signs of movement or light behind it. She imagined sticking her foot in that darkness and losing it completely, having it lopped off, sealed and cauterized before she even knew what had happened. She had a quick flash to a horror movie she and Sam had watched at Halloween, after they'd handed out mini candy bars at the front door. In the film, the woman, one of those very blonde women that populate horror movies, had stuck her hand through a patch of darkness on the other side of a black wall. (Claire couldn't remember exactly what the wall had been—an energy field? A door into another dimension?) When the woman wrenched her arm free, it was a stump haemorrhaging blood. That night, the image had been almost funny, so unlikely and baroque that both Claire and Sam had burst into laughter at the sight of the girl screaming, her arm spraying like a garden hose. Later, Claire had dreamed about that scene, and still did—only it was her arm plunging through that wall, her blood everywhere.

Sam touched the edges lightly with his hand. "No glass," he said. "It's safe."

"But I can't fit—I'm fatter than you."

Sam laughed. "I'll go first—if I can fit through, then you can fit through. We're the same size exactly." He got down on his hands and knees, ready to climb through.

"Are you sure he said a basement window?" Claire asked.

Basements were damp and filled with god knows what. Her mother kept boxes full of jelly jars in the basement, jars so covered in dust and muck that Claire couldn't imagine anyone would ever have the desire to scrub them clean and use them. What if this basement was filled with something like that—glass, old clothes, piles of newspapers?

"Yeah," Sam said. He had already put one leg through the window, then the other. He was on his stomach, sliding down the hole, half of his body already gone. He looked up at her, smiling. She imagined him cut off at the waist, the darkness swallowing him without him even knowing it.

"I'll see if anyone's down here," he said.

Later, Claire would think that this was the crucial moment—this was where she could have stopped him. She could have shouted *wait*. She could have said, *Let's just go home and watch a movie.* They could have watched *Heathers* for the fifteenth time and stolen a little bit of their parents' booze from the liquor cabinet, that cinnamon kind that tasted like candy and made Claire's throat burn, and they could have fallen asleep on the couch. She could have made him change his mind. He would have heard the fear in her voice and he would have given in. He might have sighed and tried to convince her, but he would have given in. He might even have been a little angry that his sister was such a chicken, but he would have given in.

But she didn't say anything except *okay*. She remembered the stories of the women who had burned to death in the basement. She imagined Sam falling down into a pile of dry bones in little Donna Reed dresses and perfect clicking pumps. But still, she said, *okay*.

"I'll be right back." He pushed himself down the hole until she could only see his white fingers on the edge of the window. Then he let go.

Immediately, she knew that something was wrong, though he gave only a brief, sharp shout—the breath must have been knocked out of him when he hit. The fall had been too heavy, too long, and she had heard a tearing sound of something hard breaking through something soft, like a hammer smashing the armrest of an easy chair, splitting the fabric.

Claire went to the window, crouched on the ground. She pushed her face into the hole, but she could not see anything.

"Sam! Are you there? Are you okay?"

She heard something move, a groan. She could hear breathing—a liquid, laboured wheezing, a sound like Mikey Dunbar made when he had asthma attacks during gym class and had to go to the bleachers and suck on a plastic inhaler.

"Sam!" Her voice was shrill and bounded into the basement. The air from the window was warm and smelled faintly of old paper—like the piles of *Life* magazines that Claire's mother kept in the pantry until they tipped and spilled on the floor, and she made their father box them up and put them up in the attic.

"I'm here," Sam said. He couldn't shout—his voice was choked, wetly wheezing.

"What happened?" She wished that she could see him—if she could, she'd know that he would be all right. But she wanted to get away from the window, too, as far away from that black square as she could. The cooling air around her seemed electrified, filled with tiny fingers and filaments, needles that kept her skin sensitive and prickling. But Sam was down there, still breathing. She would go down that hole to where he was, if he asked her to.

"I fell on something," he said. His voice was small and strained, and she had to lean into the darkness to hear him.

"I fell on something and it hurts. I can't breathe. I need help."

"I'll come down," Claire said. "I'll come and get you."

"Don't come down!" Sam tried to shout, but the words gargled in his throat. *Blood in his mouth*, Claire thought. She could almost taste it in hers, too.

"Okay," she shouted. "What should I do?"

"Get somebody," he said. He could hardly speak, he was breathing so thickly.

"I don't want to leave you," she said. She was crying now. She could see nothing down there, not even a glint from his watch or the white of his tennis shoes. Though it was useless, she ran the scene of him going through the window over and over again in her head. It was only minutes ago. It seemed unfair that she couldn't just go back and fix it, couldn't just step back and go home. For the first time, she was aware of the ridiculous forward motion of events—it had been so recent, it seemed that she should be able to go back and stop it. But things moved in only one direction.

"Go." He gurgled and sputtered. She breathed in deeply—she smelled something sweet and sickening, like a slice of cake left out overnight after a birthday party.

She pushed away from the window, rocking up onto her feet. "I'm going to go now. I'm going to be back. You're going to be okay."

She didn't stay to hear his response. She didn't want to hear his rasping wheeze again. She imagined the sample human body in her science classroom in school, the plastic model with removable parts. The model's lungs were bright pink. You could take them in your hands and split them open at the hinge and see the chambers and routes inside. She closed her eyes, said Sam's name aloud twice, and then she ran.

She ran back home, down the sidewalks they'd crossed just five minutes before, down the streets of identical houses, the automatic porch lights flicking on in turn as she passed, past cars like quiet animals in the driveways, windows and doors firmly shut. She ran as fast as she had ever run before, her lungs burning, inhaling and exhaling in hitches. She thought her chest might fly open from her violent breathing. She pumped her arms and legs, telling herself *I must get home*. She didn't think about the feeling at her back, the great blackness. It echoed. It bounced and repeated, screaming in her ear. It was alone.

At first, whatever slept there didn't know about the blood, if you could call what it did *knowing*. It only woke with the same thought it had fallen asleep with—*I will never leave here, look what he has done to me, Jesus Christ I can't breathe, oh God, Please don't let it*—and, of course, the anger that came with it, the red, suffocating colour and pressure.

The energy gathered force, gathered language, as the blood flowed on the ground, filled the air with its mineral stench.

The boy was dying. Life leaked from him, filled the room with its humming, its bouncing and turning and agony of being freed from the container that kept it. It flowed into the thing that said *I will never leave*. And it flowed into the anger and the cry and the cracked skulls and the fire travelling up their hair; the one who was burned alive and the one who died before she understood what she had done wrong or why; the one who was crushed and the one who was killed and never found—the little girl in her Easter dress who had gone too far to find eggs. She'd crouched down to the ground to better see something shining, and then all had gone black and her mouth said something she did not understand and she was gone and in this pool with the others, with the voices. Whatever they were now, whatever she was now, the boy's blood had joined it, a big throbbing thing, and it had gained another, and the anger was louder.

Claire ran through the front door, not bothering to close it behind her. She went to her parents' room and shook their sleeping shoulders. It felt wrong to touch them while they were sleeping—her mother not wearing her usual mascara, her eyes pinkish and bare; her father in his black socks, no shoes. They were still sick, wheezing and whistling as they woke, coughing into their fists. She had planned to calmly tell them *Sam fell*, but she could not help herself from crying, her words slurring and coming in gulps and coughs.

"What's wrong?" her mother asked.

"It's Sam. Sam fell. We were at the slate factory, just to see what was going on, and he fell into the basement."

Her father got out of bed and went to the telephone to call an ambulance, and her mother pulled on a pair of jeans and a sweater over her slip. Her father said *thank you* and hung up. Claire watched them moving normally, putting on shoes, clicking watches on their wrists. If they could act normally, then maybe nothing was really wrong. Then they all got in the car to go back.

The road was completely empty as they drove to the factory. Claire watched the dark windows as they passed. The people behind those windows were sleeping in their beds, nothing wrong, nothing jerking them from sleep and making them drive to a deserted part of town to look down into a basement window. She wished to be in any other house, with any other parents, to have her brother safe in the next room, and to have only the next day to worry about.

She waited for them to panic, for them to shout at her, but they sat silently. Her father switched on the radio and something slow, a plodding piano melody, filled the car. He tapped his fingers on the steering wheel as though the music had a beat. Her mother switched it off.

They were so calm they made her squirm in her seat. Wasn't it time to be worried? She sat on her hands and chewed the inside of her mouth until she broke the skin and tasted salt. The blood made her think of Sam, and she swallowed.

The ambulance had arrived before them. When they pulled up and parked in the gravel parking lot, the paramedics were already wheeling Sam out. The door to the factory was open.

Claire looked inside, hoping to see something, some evidence that Sam had not been alone—that she hadn't left him by himself in the dark, bleeding—but there was nothing. The open door revealed only more darkness, pure, without even the dim trailing of a streetlight to reach it.

Sam was dying. He would not leave the ambulance alive. She had not yet entertained the idea, but it hit her like a punch to the gut. It was a sudden realignment of her understanding, like when she learned to ride her bike and suddenly knew exactly how to balance her body. She ran to Sam as they wheeled him into the ambulance, her parents behind her. She hardly registered their footsteps. She tripped on a boulder and almost fell onto the stretcher, but one of the paramedics caught her by the sweater-sleeve.

"Is he okay?" Claire shouted at the paramedic. She was happy to see a little spray of spit fly up into the young man's face. The sympathy in his face infuriated her. He did not blink or wipe his cheek. She clenched her fists at her side and shouted again.

"Is he going to be all right?"

The paramedic was utterly unable to hide his pity. She looked past him to Sam's ashy face poking above the white sheet. She couldn't see him well enough to see if his eyes were opened or closed. Blood speckled his face. She looked away.

The paramedic composed himself for her. She could see that he was not going to tell her the truth.

"We are going to take him to the hospital, okay? We don't know anything yet."

He turned and they put Sam into the ambulance. *Loaded* was the word that came to mind, as they rolled him up the ramp, his weight leaden as a sack of potatoes. He didn't speak. He didn't move.

* * *

She rode to the hospital with her father—her mother went in the ambulance.

It should have been me, Claire wanted to say, but there was no point. It didn't matter who it should have been. Her father drove slowly and carefully. She got the sense that he was trying to protect her by pretending that everything was normal.

Her father said that Sam would be better, not to worry, not to worry at all.

"He just had a fall, is all."

Her father paused, probably noting the accidental rhyme. He had always been quick to notice puns, to delight in accidental repetitions and malapropisms. Claire watched him, already grieving the change that would come over him soon. No more waking early to circle the typos in the local paper, to look at the *funny papers*. He'd be a different kind of person soon. They all would. She mourned him even as he spoke.

"The doctors can work miracles these days," he said. "But Sam won't need a miracle."

He switched on the radio, a clatter of violins and swells of brass.

Claire pressed her hot face against the passenger side window, cool and greasy against her skin. She wanted the night to be over as soon as possible. She wanted it to be over so that the next day could come, and then the next one, so that weeks and then months would be between this day and the others.

But she wanted time to stop, too, that grinding forward motion. As long as they didn't reach the hospital, Sam was still alive. If they just kept driving and never arrived, they would never know, and so Sam would still be here.

When they reached the hospital parking lot, Claire knew. As they pulled into a space near the entrance and parked, Claire saw her mother open the thick glass doors and run from the lobby, crying, screaming Sam's name. She'd been waiting for them. Claire went down on her hands and knees and threw up, right there in the compact car parking spot. She observed the blotches of oil on the ground and a stray Hershey's bar wrapper, dirty and plastered against the curb. She vomited so violently that it made her cry and cough and she could hardly breathe. Nobody went to her to pull back her hair or help her up. It was better that way. It was good for her to practise being alone.

"He's gone," she heard her mother crying into her father's sweater. "He was gone before they could do anything. He was gone by the time we got here," she said.

Though Claire was on her hands and knees, trying to get the vomit from her lips so that she could join her parents, could at least stand with them and cry and let them hold her as if she were a child, she could hear something in her mother's voice—a little silver blade of blame. She could feel it touch her. She could feel it pressing against the inside of her skull like a migraine.

Samuel Thomas Martin died on September 15th, 1993, from major blood loss, injury to the lungs and other internal organs, and severe head trauma. At the time, it had seemed important to Claire to know the details of what had happened. Knowing the names of his injuries meant they could be written down on paper or spoken, and Claire could keep them with her and they would not escape her. If she had possession of the correct words, she had control over them. When somebody asked what had happened (though few people did—the paper had covered it, and nobody knew what more to say or how to handle whatever sadness might be stirred but the question), she said it just like that—he died from blood loss and lung damage and severe head trauma.

When he fell through the window, he had fallen directly on

a long, sharp piece of a broken loom, left down in the basement after the textile factory went out of business. It had pierced his ribs, his right lung, and had cracked his breastbone. It had not punctured his heart, but his head had crashed against the metal base of the machine and his skull had been fractured. Even as he had gasped and wheezed for Claire to find help, blood was filling his skull, his lungs, draining him as it blued and purpled his lips and under his eyes. Claire had not seen this, but she imagined it. She imagined it every night.

"I know there are very few things that could bring you comfort now," the doctor had said, his blue eyes bright and interested, "but your son wouldn't have made it, even if we had gotten there immediately. There was just too much damage."

"I am sorry for your loss," he added as an afterthought. He couldn't help it. He wasn't intentionally cruel. It simply didn't matter to him.

Claire left as the doctor informed her father of all of the ways that Sam's intact organs could benefit people still alive. She stood in the glass hallway between the waiting room and the outer doors. She tried to slow her breathing; she felt that she had been breathing heavily, panting, since she had run home, and that she'd never really caught her breath. Later, she regretted leaving her father alone in that room. At the time her mother was somewhere else in the hospital—Claire didn't think it strange in the moment that she wasn't there. Nothing was stranger than Sam not being there, and nothing seemed to be in its right place. But she wished her father hadn't been forced to sign papers alone, to offer Sam's eyes and kidneys, all of his young parts, and to agree that Sam no longer needed them.

She didn't care about people who were still alive.

They had taken away his body and she didn't know where it had gone.

The room Sam had been wheeled into was empty now. She

had not seen him, though her father and mother had, before they took him away. She couldn't bear to see him that way, though later, she regretted that decision. It had happened so quickly, as though they were afraid to let his dead body stay and infect everyone else with its stillness.

She never told her parents—it would make her seem too selfish—but it was the quiet in her head that she mourned the most, at least that first day. Later, she would miss Sam himself, as he was now separate from her (as much as she couldn't understand him being separate from her), but that day, she missed the Sam in her head.

In the first few weeks, Claire often closed her eyes and tried to conjure up his face in the dark. It didn't work, not like she wanted; his face appeared hazy, unformed. She had to consult photographs to remember exactly which side of his hair rose in a cowlick, which eye was smaller than the other.

That's what other people did who had family members who had died. They would make a scrapbook of photos and try to remember. It seemed a failure of character that Sam was leaving her mind, that she had to try to recall him. If she had loved him enough, she wouldn't forget essential things, like his favourite ice cream flavour or rock band.

This must be what it's like to be a regular person, she thought as she listened to the silence in the next room. The silence in her head was like the whirring of air inside a seashell.

II

JULY, PRESENT DAY

Justin discovered the factory by chance on his way back from a conference in Keene, New Hampshire, where he'd spoken with a store manager about rampant theft at the Beans stores in the area; he had given a PowerPoint presentation about preventing theft instead of prosecuting it. Justin had a PowerPoint for almost everything he might possibly have to say to his employees. He had once lamented the rise of PowerPoint presentations as a replacement for actual discussions, but now he welcomed the distance they provided. If an idea, command, or even warning was delivered through a computer program with a nice blue border and a few pictures to accompany it, then it was less frightening, less personal. He disliked the disciplinary aspects of his job—firing people gave him stomach cramps, made him feel like a complete and utter asshole. He couldn't really blame twenty-something high-school dropouts being paid eight dollars an hour for stealing. The world probably did owe them something. But he couldn't allow them to steal from him.

Scenic Route 9 went through Farmington, a sweet, small, old town, dotted with those green-tinted plaques and monuments erected at the scenes of even the most unimportant events of the Revolutionary War, such as the spot where General such-and-such rested his horse, or where some rag-tag local militia had hoarded their muskets. This town was particularly beautiful, though—it had a classic white church at the centre, original brick buildings and streets paved in cobblestone, and old, broken-down factory buildings down by the river, where a waterwheel had once powered them.

Most were vacant, though some were still in fine condition—*they could be remodelled*, Justin thought as he passed, made into little mini-malls filled with high-end specialty stores, establishments that weren't seen as tacky or trashy or a blight on the landscape.

He was always thinking of ways to use empty spaces. This was something Gary, his supervisor, admired about him.

"You're always thinking, aren't you?" Gary had once asked. He pointed at Justin, right in front of the five other New England and Upstate New York district managers during a staff meeting. This embarrassed Justin. He didn't like to be singled out.

"Everyone is always thinking," Justin had replied. "Only some people don't say everything they're thinking the moment they think it."

Everyone in the room had laughed mildly, in that way people laugh at jokes that are not funny. Justin had successfully deflected the compliment. As the meeting ended, Gary asked him to take a small stipend to scout out a new Beans location for their New England expansion.

"You really care about the company," he'd said. "We see that, and we want to reward it."

Corporate had discussed creating a branch in southern Vermont—most of the population was centred in the North, but the Southern parts of the state bordered many highly populated areas in Massachusetts and New York, so they got a great deal of tourist traffic. Justin had taken his time on the way back, scouting out locations, but there had been nothing promising until now. The factories in Farmington were set along the one major scenic highway out of Farmington and to Albany, a highway advertised as one of the most beautiful routes in the entirety of New England. But there were few establishments along the way except a few gift shops selling maple syrup and t-shirts. *So much potential here*, Justin thought. It almost made him angry, how undeveloped the place was. Didn't people know that empty spaces were made to be filled?

Justin continued past the place where the town's sidewalks ended and the sparsely populated countryside began. It consisted of houses that had once been beautiful but now sat nestled amongst overgrown shrubs and untended front yards.

As he reached the town's limit, where the scenic highway grew wild and then, across the New York state border, become two-laned again, he slowed and made a U-turn.

He had a hunch.

He drove back to Farmington and parked on the gravel lot of the very last factory, a two-storey building shingled in dull but reflective slate, its grey blending with the choppy, high river behind it.

The door was locked shut with a padlock that hung from a heavy chain. The chain, suddenly, brought him back home, to his childhood. He'd had a dog when he was six or seven—Zeus, a mix between husky and something else, a beautiful mutt— that his mother chained to a tree near his doghouse because he ran away whenever he was set free. The chain was thick, heavy, and Justin had pitied the dog, having to carry it around on his neck all of the time. He couldn't remember what had happened to the dog. He hoped it had gotten free, but that was unlikely. It had probably died, like most of their pets, and he had probably buried it in the backyard himself, since his father's back hurt too much to shovel.

He lifted the hanging length of chain and let it fall and clang against the heavy door.

Justin walked the perimeter of the building, his shined shoes collecting a layer of dust from the gravel. The place looked renovated—some of the shingles were newer, less chipped and ragged, and the windows were sturdy and well insulated— not broken, like the glass in the windows of most abandoned buildings.

Justin saw no signs indicating who owned the place. He scrawled the name of the road in the notebook he always kept in his back pocket, in case he felt an idea coming. He believed in listening to hunches. He had read about hunches in *The Seven Secrets of Success*. He had written the seven secrets carefully in each of his college notebooks, and later made a poster to put in his office at Beans, right above his desk so he would never forget them.

It was difficult for Justin to find any information about the factory. He called several real estate companies in Farmington. They said they didn't know who owned it, or that it had belonged to an out-of-towner, that it was passed along through inheritance, that the owner had abandoned it. Justin doubted all their stories. They were told with an air of impromptu invention, a careless flinging of contradictory facts.

"It's been abandoned, like, forever," one receptionist said.

"But who abandoned it? Do you happen to have any information about that?" he asked. Justin believed he had a knack for dealing with country people, these secretaries and managers and realtors who fooled out-of-towners into renting summer homes by their shallow, algae-infested lakes, or buying over-priced rustic lawn furniture. But he understood them, too—not like the other management at Beans, most of whom had been to business school and saw their present positions as merely a rung in the inevitable ladder up and up until a comfortable retirement. Justin had grown up in a small town. When he called somebody who pronounced the word *idea* as *idear*, or referred to anything as being *upstreet*, he knew that he was speaking to his people. He could imagine himself on the other side of the telephone, a game of solitaire on the computer, cold coffee in a cup, twenty-five-dollar shoes pinching his feet. If things had gone badly, that's where he would be right now.

The woman made a humming sound like a garbage disposal. "I'm not sure about that, sir. It's been abandoned for about five, six years now. The company is gone. Not sure if they were renting or leasing or what. Not sure," she repeated.

Justin heard the sound of her typing in the background, click clack.

"Looks like the factory isn't in our database, sir. You'll have to call Johnson Realty."

Justin called Johnson Realty, who were equally evasive, though their receptionist was at least honest about his lack of forthrightness.

"I'm not sure if I can talk about that," he said. Justin heard the boy shifting gum around in his mouth. "I don't think it's officially on the market. Let me talk to my supervisor."

The phone clattered down and then distant, muffled voices rose and fell; the receptionist hadn't even put him on hold.

"Sir? Hi. I'm back. We do handle that property, sir." The voice assumed the helpful tones of professionalism, and Justin was heartened. Justin was an adherent to the Broken Window Theory, which he'd read about in some bestselling book he'd received for his birthday. It claimed that when things looked like a mess they ended up becoming a mess, because everyone realized that disorder reigned and nobody was really in charge of anything.

Order was a way to pretend that the world was not continually in danger of collapse, and when people believed this, they were less likely to destroy things. Professionalism added to this helpful illusion. It was a row of imaginary intact windows.

Justin's job was preserving order. People were relieved when they walked into a store and saw carefully piled and folded clothes, bins full of fragrant coffee beans, shelves that were dusted and painted and bore no signs of wear. It was better than therapy, he sometimes thought, to put one's own house, one's spaces, in order. Justin had never gone to therapy, but he couldn't imagine that talking to somebody about things in the past that could not be changed could possibly be more satisfying than taking something in your hands and changing it yourself.

"Excellent," Justin said. "Can you transfer me to the agent handling this property?"

With no warning, Justin was turned over to another voice—this one gruff, male, older, with a bit of a smoker's rasp.

"Gilbert," the voice said. "What can I do for you?"

"I'm curious about a certain property."

By the end of the telephone call, Justin was pleased enough to open a new bottle of wine and drink the first glass by himself. Karen, his fiancée, was at a late-night spinning class. In Justin's opinion, going from work to a class where you had to sweat and grunt in a room full of people to annoying, repetitive music seemed like yet another hellish experience that contemporary people willingly subjected themselves to, much like bikini waxing and colon cleansing. But it made Karen happy.

Justin drank his glass of wine slowly, imagining Karen on the bicycle, her hair soaked with sweat. Neither one of them were very good at relaxation. She preferred sweating, moving, and talking to sitting down. During movies, they both ate steadily, moving their hands from popcorn bucket to mouth.

Justin was terrible at holiday gatherings, where he was expected to sit down and have a conversation in front of a football game or parade or a cheese and cracker tray. He fidgeted and was easily distracted by the view from the window, no matter how meagre. He found it hard to follow conversations that drifted from pointless observation to mild interjection to second pointless observation.

But he could relax now. He had accomplished something. He felt his jaw unclench, the small muscles around his mouth— muscles that he hadn't realized were tightened—release.

The factory was available. It was not only available, but it was available at a discount, a deep discount, because the owner wanted to be rid of it—but only to the right buyer. They wanted a reputable company to take it over. The other companies that had approached them hadn't fit the bill. The location, too, made it a hard sell, according to the realtor.

But Justin disagreed. In the ten years he had been with Beans, he'd studied people. He subscribed to *Business Weekly* and read their portraits of the everyday consumer. He imagined that he knew something about the way that people made decisions. Many of the people who lived in a dying factory town like Farmington, where the only jobs were for retail workers, waitresses, mechanics, high school teachers, and bank tellers, were the kind of people who needed small luxuries, like coffee. The other people who lived there were largely wealthy retirees and college professors who worked at the nearby liberal arts school. They, too, would be attracted to Beans.

He drummed his fingers on the glass tabletop and took off his shoes. He had drunk almost half the bottle of wine by himself. Karen was a half-hour late. Justin felt his hands moving toward his mouth, his teeth closing in around the half-moon edges of his fingernails. He grabbed his cell phone and paced the room.

"Gary, it's Justin. I think I've found our Southwestern location."

"Christ, Justin, you work fast." Gary was in his car—Justin could hear the radio in the background, some voices in a cacophony of shouts. Gary liked to listen to radio shows where people with unshakable opinions disagreed violently about issues of great complexity. This kind of argument gave Justin a headache.

"So, this place is good?"

"It's good. It's a little strange—I'll have to explain the concept to you later—but the price is right, and we can do so much with the space."

When they ended the call, Justin still felt restless.

It wasn't enough. Justin needed to do something with his body, he decided, something more than looking at a book or a screen. He took off his shoes and paced the carpet in his black socks. The socks itched his feet, so he took them off and walked barefoot, feeling the plush between his toes.

He stood in the middle of the living room, wishing Karen were home. He needed somebody to reflect his success back to him. Until then, it wouldn't feel real. As much as he tried, he wasn't yet in the habit of believing in his own success.

Justin had grown up poor, the third son in a family of six, in a small town in the Adirondacks. His mother had cleaned rooms for a local hotel and for some families in the area. She had found small ways to be proud. This quality of hers saddened Justin more than her thick-soled shoes, her pants with elastic waistbands, and the baloney sandwiches she made for herself in the mornings and ate during breaks on a bench by the gas station.

She would bring him home toys that other children had left at the hotel: a G.I. Joe action figure missing one arm, a stuffed elephant, a whole set of Little Golden Books. But she had always worried about money. She shouted when he drank too much milk, or asked for second helpings of meat, or spent his quarters on gum and video games at the arcade.

"Do you know how much I worked to buy this meat?" his mother would shout when he wouldn't finish his dinner. She could point her wooden spoon at the hamburger and turn the ground cylinders of meat into money and the aches of her labour.

Justin had not forgotten how it was to have less—the tightness in his throat and shoulders when he grew out of his t-shirts, or the blisters he developed when his feet grew too large for his shoes, or the rush of blood that came to his face when he had to spend money for a school project and knew he would have to ask his mother, and that it would shame her to say no. Justin had grown up eating peanut butter and jelly sandwiches on white bread and a vast array of casseroles, such as tuna noodle with cream of mushroom soup, often punctuated with whatever canned vegetable there had been a sale on at the grocery store. He'd worn his older brothers' clothes and slept in a bed with his younger sister, Lilly, until they were both teenagers and their parents shoved another twin bed in the room so they could have their *privacy*. Even now, when he had no trouble purchasing the things he needed, Justin felt tightness in his chest when the toothpaste tube was suddenly empty.

He understood as a child that the world, at any moment, might fall apart. He had always known this. He could not remember a moment when he believed that his parents could save him from the world and its chance disasters or misfortunes. It wasn't any better for adults; if you fell behind in payments you might lose your home, you might go hungry, you might get sick and not be able to pay to fix it. These things were not impossible, and so Justin had planned for them. He kept the telephone number to DHS written in his school notebooks. He knew that it took twenty minutes to get to the closest neighbour and that they had a telephone, two cars, and were kind. If he absolutely needed to, he'd have somewhere to go.

Justin had decided that he would not be caught by accident. He wouldn't fall behind. He wouldn't stop moving forward. And now, here he was, so far ahead that he couldn't possibly go back to where he had come from. There wasn't any reason to be afraid anymore.

III

Claire worked late on Tuesdays and Wednesdays. She supervised the "Getting to Know the Computer" classes that the library held for free for anyone over the age of fifty-five who wanted to learn how to navigate the Internet, or even just open the library website to search for a book. People still sometimes asked for the card catalogue and stared, confused, when she pointed at the computer. It never ceased to surprise her how so many people could have gone through life without knowing what a mouse was or how to use it.

Claire spent most of her work days re-shelving books and magazines, checking in and checking out books, walking the floors of the library, and shooing away teenagers who used the meeting rooms and desks to eat their lunches of potato chips and soda. She was often surprised to hear her own voice out loud when she told the occasional library patron to take their feet from the desk or please throw away any drinks without lids.

Her solitary job suited her, though sometimes she was surprised by the excitement she felt when somebody asked her a question. She had once pretended to lose her way when helping a particularly handsome young man find some murder mystery series. She had known exactly which one he wanted—it was a popular paperback, the cover worn, the pages dog-eared, the kind of book that always seemed exciting from the outside, but bored her to death when she actually sat down to read it— but she'd kept him in general fiction for five minutes, asking him about his school, his life, his interests, before she chose to remember that the mysteries were all in a separate section, at the back of the library.

I'm not really like I seem right now, she wanted to tell him. She was not usually quite so desperate for human connection. Mostly, she was happy.

Claire didn't keep a journal (the idea of writing such a thing exhausted her), so she didn't have a sense of the general trajectory of her happiness throughout her life. She did not remember many times of overwhelming unhappiness (though there had been some—Sam, of course). She believed that she fulfilled a useful position in the world, one that fit her. She was not a person of great ambition—it was enough to live in a familiar town, to do even a small amount of good. So many people did less. She had very little to complain about.

Claire had worked for the Farmington library for eight years. She'd graduated from the state university with her master's in Library Sciences after an accelerated five-year degree plan. It had never occurred to her to be anything but a librarian.

It's the only way I won't be lonely, she'd often thought. A funny thing to think, she knew, but it was the truth. Just the idea being in the proximity of stacks and stacks of pages that had been read and thumbed-through, or even ignored by hundreds, if not thousands, of other people, gave her comfort. She liked thinking about how they had held each book: the people who compulsively read the cheap little paperbacks with coloured spines in the Romance section, those who thumbed through the Zane Grey collection, or the ones who checked out Salinger's Glass family stories over and over again. She liked holding each book and imagining that she had a little bit of somebody else's skin on hers, the traces of heat from their hands now in her hands. Her sense of spirituality began and ended in the library, with the memories of hands and eyes on so many pages over hundreds of years.

It was a kind of immortality to have the words you'd thought of bound up in a book, kept in a building, speaking to people long after your death. When Claire was in high school, when her reading had become *obsessive* (according to her mother, who considered all enthusiasms excessive), she would underline sentences in books that revealed something that she had felt before but had not realized that other people felt, too. Like the desire to hurt something beautiful because it was beautiful, or the sudden urge to jump from something very high because it was there and seemed to call out to be jumped from. Finding such things made her feel part of the larger world.

She often had this feeling of expansiveness when she listened to *Casey's Top 40* as a teenager. She'd lie out on the front lawn on her old quilt, moving with the shade as the day progressed, the boom box batteries so close to dead that only the FM stations would work. Sam would tease her for listening to such a goofy show, for turning up the radio when Casey began his slick, rat-a-tat routine, but she liked hearing the call-in dedications, all of those voices from far away suddenly intimate and in her ears.

The library made her feel like that: close to thousands of whispering voices.

She loved her work, but Claire knew that she had stayed in Farmington to do that work because of Sam.

After Sam's death, her life had not resumed its former shape, as the counsellors and teachers and psychologists had said it would. As everybody had promised.

This sadness will pass in time, they'd told her. *You'll never forget him, but the pain will lessen.* They assured her that everybody thought, at first, that the pain would never pass, that nothing would ever be the same, but it would. *You will snap back*, they said. One day, they said, she would wake up in the morning and not think of Sam until after breakfast. Later, maybe she wouldn't think of him until dinner, or even bedtime, while brushing her teeth. They told her this as though she should hope for such forgetfulness.

But she was not the same person. Half of the person she had been was gone.

She kept to herself. *You keep too many secrets*, her mother had said, and it was true, but not for the reasons her parents might have imagined—sex, a drinking habit, piercings that they wouldn't approve of. It was nothing like that. She did not kiss a boy until her senior year, at prom, when the guy she went with, Denny, had pressed his face against hers in the parking lot and searched for her mouth in the dark. She had been cold and tired and flush-faced from being around so many people for so long. She had let him hold himself against her until she felt tension in him, until she felt him clutching, then she had pushed him away, saying that she was cold, that she was tired, that she wanted to go home. She got a reputation for being uptight, a cock tease. She didn't mind.

As a teenager, she didn't feel comfortable in the world. She would sometimes feel struck with the awkwardness of her body, of other people's bodies—of human bodies in general—and feel an overwhelming need to climb under her desk or blankets or the dinner table and pull her arms and legs tight against her chest and stomach and become as small and compact as possible. At school, while standing in the hallway between classes, she often heard a swell of different voices amplified in her head, making a racket like a room full of people ripping sheets.

When she lost Sam, she lost her ability to be easy with people. She plodded, uncertain of how loudly to speak, how close to stand to other people, when to say hello and when not to say hello. She had forgotten how to be a regular person.

And her parents changed, too. They kept their distance from her, even as they complained about her pulling away. Sometimes, after Sam's death, when they all sat around the dinner table moving potatoes around with their forks, cutting the meat into little strips, Claire could feel her mother's eyes on her, trying to look through her, not at her, not at anything her face might be saying or doing.

She's trying to find the Sam in me, Claire would think. *She's trying to push away the Claire and get the Sam out.*

After a while, she avoided her mother as much as possible. When her mother was upset, the entire house was agitated— the hot water scalded, the floors creaked, the refrigerator groaned and made painful whirring noises. Her mother was silent, brooding, not the type to shout or openly confront anyone. Instead, she shut down her face, her eyes, and closed her lips tight. Claire never knew when she would unwittingly upset her mother. It was impossible to tell what might set her off: a broken cup, a television commercial featuring a boy and his father, a diaper commercial with a baby holding its own fat feet. Or simply Claire standing in the doorway, brushing her teeth. As she grew older, she moved quietly away from them with no open rancour, no discussion of hurt feelings, but a general sense of having lost something she never quite had to begin with.

Claire's relationship with her father was as it had been since Sam's death: he was a genial ghost, shouting hello from an easy chair where he watched public television and let the world spin around him. She came to visit on holidays and birthdays. She listened to her mother when she called, listened to her complain about the family next door that stole her mail and how the kids on the street rolled their skateboards back and forth all night, keeping her awake with the grind of the hard wheels against the concrete.

Claire was happy to listen to her complaints—they didn't require a complicated response, or for her to talk about her own life. They only required noises of agreement. When her parents asked how she was, she said *fine* and that was that. They didn't seem to want more. Or maybe they didn't believe that there was more. Claire did not blame them for an uncharitable assumption. From the outside, her life seemed to follow very steady, even lines.

She wasn't the girl who flirted anymore. She wasn't the girl who had teased Archie about weed (and what had happened to Archie, anyway? She'd heard he'd gotten married, joined the military, and then he'd disappeared). She hadn't been that person in so long she remembered only vaguely what it was like. She missed that Claire, the one with her bangs feathered up, her enormous hot-pink t-shirts tied at her hip. Claire didn't go to bars. She didn't join clubs. She didn't have close friends— just a few men she had dated and said hello to in the grocery store and her co-workers. She had lived with two men in town. She saw them sometimes, from afar, and often waved, or even walked up to them to have a conversation that skipped lightly across the surface of their history. She was grateful that she had never seen one of them with another woman. Or a child.

In Farmington, people knew her history. She couldn't pretend that she was whole and normal. When they looked at her, particularly people her own age and her parents' age, they knew something about her—they were remembering Sam when they looked at her. They could feel the absence and pitied her for it.

Maybe even the ones who had never known Sam, who didn't know anything about her, could tell. She imagined she carried the loss with her like a scent.

She thought sometimes that things would have been better if she had left, but Farmington was the only place she knew well, and it gave her comfort to see the same rows of trees, the same gravestones leaning in the back of the Old Farmington graveyard, their dates and names worn almost flat.

Leaving would mean leaving Sam, and she couldn't do that, though she knew he was only a body in a box now (she couldn't follow this line of thought past those words—Sam in the grave-yard, Sam's body reduced to bone and leather and hair) and he didn't even know that she was still here, keeping a promise she had never given and that he never would have asked her to make.

She felt, in a small way, that she had let Sam down. Though she didn't believe in the afterlife, in spirits watching the people below from the bleachers of heaven, amused at their continual fuck-ups and self-created miseries, she often felt that he was watching her and disapproving of the smallness of her life.

As soon as Claire finished her shift, she went directly home to eat dinner alone. When she looked in the mirror (which she didn't do very often), she had a feeling of helplessness at the sight of her face changing—she wasn't old, she wasn't unattract-ive, but she was losing her youth, her years of being pretty with-out trying. She had wasted her twenties reading books in bed. She had wasted time with men that she did not love, and who did not love her, but served as a person to fill the empty place in her head for a while.

She knew the problem: there wasn't enough of her to love. Sam had occupied half of her mind, and with him gone there was too much empty space. Her thoughts rattled and her per-sonality had become dislodged, unanchored. It had no shape, no definition. She knew that she could be funny, charming even, but that at the centre of her, there was something essential missing, something that other people had all on their own but that Sam had taken away from her.

* * *

In late July, she dreamed about Sam for the first time in a very long time. It had been so long that when she woke, her heart was beating so quick and hard that she was afraid she might be having a panic attack. She woke cold, her window open, though she never slept with the window open. She had left her window open at night once as a child and had woken to a bird on her dresser, shrieking, not singing. After that, the idea of being surprised by nature kept her in stuffy, air-less rooms.

Sun flooded her carpet; the air on her face was clean. It would have been a beautiful way to wake up if she'd planned it. But she hadn't, and so she was afraid. Maybe there was a robin in her closet, a spider in her underwear drawer, a man with a knife under the bed come to take her collection of Jeff Buckley albums and self-help books.

She laughed at herself and threw the covers off. She would not be afraid of ridiculous things. She wasn't worth stealing from. She had nothing anyone else could possibly want.

Claire showed up at the library at eight every morning to lay out the morning papers, change the old magazines, and shelve the books that had been left in the drop box before opening at nine. She switched on each computer, one after the other, and they wheezed to life with one great breath. She walked the floors and picked up stray pieces of paper and receipts, pushed the stacks of books back against the book-shelf walls and flush to the left or right, each book pressed tight against the one before it.

That morning, as she put the *Farmington Banner* on the reading room table, she saw a headline that made her stop and put down the pile of books she'd been holding.

Beans Plan to Buy and Renovate
The New England Textiles Factory

A company named Beans was in the process of buying the factory to convert it to a boutique store, offering a coffee and snack bar, chocolates, and gourmet gifts. The district manager, who would personally oversee the design, explained that they would hire over twenty-five employees from the area and would give visitors "yet another reason to come to Farmington."

Claire laughed at this quote—there really weren't any reasons to come to Farmington to begin with. A bunch of statues marking minor points in the Revolutionary War, the Farmington Monument, pointing upward like an enormous phallic symbol in the sky, and a college so expensive that hardly any locals could actually attend it. Claire loved her town, but she knew its weaknesses, and she knew flattery when she read it.

She set down the paper. They were going to re-open the factory.

Claire folded her hands in her lap and stared at the brick wall across from her, at the poster of Oprah holding a Toni Morrison book, encouraging people to read. Oprah smiled widely, as though really everything that went wrong could be solved with a good book, with a positive thought, with the right mantra or attitude toward unhappiness.

There isn't anything I can do about it. Claire said this aloud. The empty library creaked and echoed back to her. It seemed the most occupied when empty, all the small noises that much more amplified, its high ceilings throwing down each small sound. *I can't stop them.*

After Sam's death, the idea of even walking past the factory, and later driving past it, made Claire short of breath, as though the muscles in her throat protested even if her voice couldn't.

Five years after Sam's death, the factory had re-opened. It had been converted into a battery factory, completely renovated. She had gone once to look—the only time she'd done so. She'd crouched down to see through the narrow basement windows along the ground. They were smaller than she remembered; she wouldn't have been able to fit through one now. She saw only boxes full of unrecognizable things and some large machines covered with sheets.

The battery factory had left town after only a few years. Unlike most other businesses and factories in town, it had not left because of economic downturn; it left because people could no longer stand working there. The employees reported nightmares, terrible headaches that no medication could cure. Their doctors prescribed them Vicodin, painkillers that made them woozy and forgetful. One woman caught her hand in a conveyor belt while in a Vicodin daze and lost the tip of her finger. Another woman fainted in the bathroom and cracked her head on the tiles. Her co-workers found her in a pool of blood. She didn't die—it was only a minor bump—but the accidents and illnesses had driven away workers, which had in turn driven the company out of the town. The factory had been empty now for about ten years.

Based on what she'd heard, teenagers went there to smoke weed or have sex, various indigent people slept there, and the windows were probably broken—it was probably filled with beer bottles, slack, sticky condoms, and soiled blankets. But she couldn't imagine it that way. She could only imagine it empty and dusty and Sam down in the basement, calling to her.

Claire didn't know who owned the factory, though as a librarian she knew much more than most people about the inner workings of the town. She knew all of the members of the Farmington Historical Society—ancient men and women, their papery hands moving over dusty photographs, their lives devoted to keeping every record of Farmington history filed neatly in its proper place in the archive room on the top floor of the library. It seemed strange to her that she didn't know.

Perhaps people didn't let her in on information that might upset her.

Claire folded the paper and placed it at the centre of the table. She finished putting away the books and opened the doors at nine o'clock sharp. A group of library regulars were outside, seated on the front bench and on the concrete perimeter that circled a small green area in front of the library. They were teenagers—bookish ones who didn't have friends, most wearing black, baggy clothes, listening to tiny earbuds—and older men and women who brought big sheaths of notebook paper and plastic bags full of notes and pored over books all day, researching something that only they understood, probably, or writing epics, manifestos, or historical volumes that would end up in boxes in their basement only to be eventually thrown away by bewildered relatives.

She liked them all. They were trying to uncover information, to formulate theories, to find God—to do something crazy and disconnected from the everyday world of waking, driving, eating, and sleeping. Claire wished she were brave enough to be more like them.

Claire shelved books and smiled at the regulars, nodded at the teenagers with their heavy backpacks and nervous, downcast eyes. She wanted them to know that she was friendly. At that age, they imagined that everyone was looking at them, laughing at the books in their bags, at their attempts at meeting or resisting some current trend (inside-out sweatshirts, Claire had noticed, was the latest). She wanted them to believe that she understood how it was to be a person at the margins of something larger, a person who was not quite recognized as real.

IV

AUGUST

Justin drove to Farmington alone. He brought along music that Karen would never let him listen to, like Steve Reich's *Different Trains*, which she said sounded like a skipping record backed by an orchestra endlessly tuning its instruments.

As Justin drove, he thought about the eagerness with which Karen had met the news that he was leaving for a long weekend. She'd kissed him enthusiastically that morning, still dressed in her nightgown. She'd hugged him hard and ran to the kitchen to get him a bag of snack mix that she had purchased for the occasion. She presented it to him proudly. Karen came from a family so wealthy that before going to college, she had never gone to a grocery store, and even then avoided chores that involved choosing and purchasing small household items. Justin did the shopping. The first and only time she'd done the shopping she'd come home with a loaf of French bread, an enormous triangle of triple cream brie, and a box of old-fashioned liquorice, bitter and sticky in its paper bag. She had looked so proud that he hadn't had the heart to critique her. From then on, he brought home groceries after work.

She likes me better when I'm leaving, he thought. *She's sleeping with somebody else.* Justin felt this was true, though he had no concrete proof, only a feeling that he did not quite meet expectations that somebody else had exceeded. He had once taken a test in *Cosmo* magazine while waiting for his dentist. It was titled "Twenty Signs Your Man is Cheating," and Karen had met eighteen of them. She had met signs that he hadn't even known were signs, such as a desire to try new sexual positions. He'd thought this was a good thing, but afterward looked upon her experiments with suspicion.

He imagined her home now, dressed after a shower, flipping through television channels or *Vogue Italia.* No, Justin thought, he should be more charitable to Karen. She could be doing something more substantial. She liked to paint with watercolours—wet little scenes from the kitchen window, quite beautiful in their formless, bleeding way. She was going through a phase where she'd paint the same scene out the window at different times of day.

Her paintings hung all over the apartment, even in the bathroom, where they rippled and curled from the humidity and the paint left faint streaks down the white walls. She had gotten her BFA in art and had always intended to do something with it. But she and Justin had started dating just after her graduation, when she was a temp at Beans' eastern headquarters, and she hadn't quite recovered her enthusiasm for art post-graduation. She couldn't gather her ideas; she couldn't concentrate. Justin told her that he was sure it was only an adjustment period. All artists need to recharge. So she painted her watercolours and waited for her inspiration to come back.

Justin imagined her in front of an enormous canvas, one of the canvases she had bought and kept in the attic—five canvases leaning against each other, their exposed edges dusty. Maybe she'd had an idea. Maybe she was painting her masterpiece.

But maybe she had never gotten dressed that morning. Maybe she had waited by the window, lighting a cigarette. He knew she sometimes smoked; the smell drove him crazy and she carried it in her hair and clothes for days. She might be smoking by the window, her hands nervously picking at a pull in her robe, until she saw a car drive up and a man emerge from the driver's side. She'd rush to the door to meet him, wrapping her arms around him, pressing her head to his chest. *He's finally gone*, she'd murmur into this man's shirt. *He finally gave us a weekend alone.*

Justin tried to focus on the road before him, a twisting, treacherous thing carved into the side of a mountain. It had come up quickly after a long stretch of flat, featureless highway. As he slowed and struggled up a hill, his economy car made small, complaining sounds. Other cars and trucks behind him sailed easily past, and he slowed to let them.

Justin was on his way to meet with the owner of the factory in Farmington and take a tour of the building. He imagined the worst—the foundations impossibly cracked with no possibility of getting the place up to code, water damage, fire damage. He prepared himself for the possibility that it wouldn't work.

After he ended the winding, downward portion of the mountain and wiped the sweat from his palms, he reached into his pocket and touched his cell phone. He pushed the speed dial for home. He tried to hum along with the sound of Reich's repeating screams of violin, as if to prove Karen wrong from miles away.

"Hello?" Karen answered quickly. Maybe she was expecting a call.

Justin paused for a beat, listening for background noise. Nothing. No music, no television.

"Hi sweetie. It's me, Justin."

"Oh, hi, Justin." Her voice fell from alertness to boredom. "Did you forget something?"

Justin paused. He had forgotten to create a legitimate reason for calling. *Calling just to hear your voice* was absurd—he had never done such a thing before.

"I was just calling to see if I left my address book on the kitchen table. I'm on the road now, so I can't check, but I'm afraid I might have. Would you mind checking for me?"

"Okay," she said, and set the phone down on the counter. He heard the clatter and reverberation. As he listened, knowing that she would come back empty handed (he could see his address book on the passenger seat next to his laptop and the unopened bag of Chex Mix), he thought he could hear the faint sounds of conversation. *Maybe it's the TV*, he thought. But the sounds were mumbling, erratic, not like that rat-a-tat of sitcom talk, the punctuation of laughing or clapping or music. As he was still trying to make out the sounds, he heard the phone scrape across the table.

"It's not here," Karen said. "I guess you brought it with you."

"I guess so," Justin said. "Thank you very much for looking for it."

"Of course," she said. "It's not a problem."

Justin imagined he could hear her rolling her eyes, tapping her toes, doodling on the pad of paper they kept on the table for messages.

"I'll see you on Tuesday," he said.

"Awesome," she said. This was her usual exclamation, one so familiar that it had come to mean exactly the opposite of its dictionary definition. "Be careful," she said.

"Love you."

"You too," she said. "Goodbye."

By the time that Justin arrived at the factory, he had put his Karen troubles away in their own little folder in his mind. He even imagined it that way, as if his brain was a big filing cabinet, neatly labelled. He had learned this trick at a company retreat. That day he'd also been forced to take part in a drum circle and get a massage from a woman with magenta hair who had told him about his aura (tinged with black, she'd said, though she had not elaborated). But nothing else had stuck with him as much as the exercise in visualizing one's life as a manageable set of folders. "The room might be enormous, and there might be dozens and dozens of cabinets and folders, but you will always find the one you need," the workshop leader had said. "And whenever you need to set an emotion aside, you can go to the right folder and put those feelings away until later, when you can deal with them."

His childhood, from birth through age ten, was in its own cabinet; his teenage years filled almost three (each drawer labelled with an age, and within each drawer, folders marked with events—first kiss, braces, first time starting on the basketball team, first major sexual humiliation); and his adult life filled many more. Karen had her own drawer. He imagined putting away her file, slipping her photograph in a manila folder and shutting the drawer. He breathed deeply. He was ready.

He pulled into the factory parking lot, the new gravel popping crisply beneath his wheels. There was an enormous red truck in the driveway, mud-stained, and a man in a baseball cap wearing flannels, dark jeans, and brown work boots leaned against the passenger door, watching Justin as he drove in and parked crookedly next to the truck.

"You must be Mr. Graves," Justin said. He offered his hand and Graves took it. He had a cold, tough hand, hard bumps where callouses bloomed on his palm. Justin used to have callouses like that, when he was younger, but not anymore. He was aware of his soft hands, his clean fingernails.

"And you must be Justin." Graves squinted and motioned to the factory. "So your company wants to buy this old place?"

"We certainly do, sir."

Mr. Graves shook his head. "All right then. I guess you'll want to take a look."

Justin nodded. "Lead the way."

Graves unlocked the deadbolt hanging from a knotted chain laced through the door handles. He turned the knob and pushed the door open. Justin blinked and pinched his nose to hold back a sneeze. He could see nothing but a thick fog of dust.

"I brought my flashlight," Graves said, rooting around in the large apron-like pockets of his flannel jacket. He took out a small flashlight and flicked it on, the light bobbing around in the dusty, still room for a few seconds as he adjusted it so that it shone in a wide swath.

Justin had once been afraid of the dark, as many children are, but he had been particularly ashamed of this fear. It had been visceral, enough to make him cry and run to his mother, something he loathed to do. He had never told anyone about it (he didn't believe in psychiatrists, or psychiatric medicine— most people he knew who went to counselling ended up crazier than they'd been before they started). He had mostly gotten over it once he turned ten or eleven, but the memory of the fear still came back to him sometimes when he stepped into a dark room. He could remember the way his stomach would feel sick and empty, how he would have the urge to curl his body around that sickness, to tighten up in a ball and close his eyes to keep anything crawling and clutching in the dark out by contracting his muscles.

Mr. Graves flashed the light around the room, narrating as they walked.

"This here is the main work floor," he said. "This is where they used to have sewing machines back when this was a textile factory. Then the battery factory was here and they took out the machines and put in conveyor belts and whatnot, put them all in the basement. Mess down there. Kid fell down there years ago and died. Tragedy, but no company liability—the kid broke in and fell. Probably drunk or high or something."

Justin nodded, as though this was just another fact in a long line of similarly pleasant and pointless facts, though he could see his own body falling through a basement window (he imagined himself being sucked down the hole like bath water down a drain).

Graves shook the flashlight at a jumble of machinery, most of it halfway disassembled, overturned, or clearly broken. "You'll have to get all that hauled out," he said. He shook the light up and down the jumble, illuminating wires, springs, and a telephone receiver, its cord severed from the base.

"It's a good space," Graves said. "Nice and big. You could do whatever you want with it."

"Yes," Justin said, clearing his throat. The dust thickened in his lungs and nose. "What's wrong with the windows?" he asked, clearing his throat again. "Can we get some light in here?"

Graves shined his light at the rectangles of dull fabric and plastic that covered the glass.

"It's just the shades down," he said. "I was just about to do that. I'll do it now, if you want."

Justin nodded again, pointlessly, as Graves couldn't see him. He felt again like a frightened child wheezing in the dark, fists tight, a hard knot of muscle and bone under his blankets, in his dark room where he could smell the wood smoke curling up from between the imperfect seams of the kitchen woodstove. If he crawled out of bed barefoot and sniffling, his wet and snot-sticky hands balled at his thighs, and went to his parents' room, he was just as likely to be shooed away as he was to be let into the bed and held. He never knew which it would be.

Graves, though not much older than Justin, seemed like somebody's father—a man who didn't have time to be afraid or panicked in the dark.

As Graves pulled down on the shades and let them snap back up around their cylinders, the room grew lighter. Justin saw that the room was indeed almost bare—it had been gutted, and only the leftover, unnecessary things that weren't worth the effort of packing remained: telephones tangled in their wires, paperclips, littered equipment that Justin couldn't identify. But the room was enormous, high ceilinged, the floor relatively empty. It was everything that he had hoped for.

"This is amazing," Justin said. When he swallowed and breathed in slowly, deeply, he could hold down the sense of being slowly suffocated.

Graves nodded and switched off his flashlight. "It's a good space, no doubt." He put his hands in his pockets.

"So why hasn't anybody else bought it?"

Graves hesitated for a moment as he fumbled while putting the flashlight back in one of the many hidden pockets of his jacket.

"Oh, I suppose it's because all the factories are moving out of here anyways." He jerked his head to the right. Justin could see, through the dirty window, the bulk of another empty factory building, its roof bowed and rotting, windows broken and jagged, the edges of glass glinting in the afternoon light. Justin looked around the factory—none of the windows had been broken, or if they had, they'd been repaired. And no graffiti inside, no signs of squatters with dirty sleeping bags, beer cans, rotten fast food wrappers.

"That's true," Justin said, "but this building is different than the others—it's beautiful, for one thing. How old is it?"

Graves looked up at the ceiling. "Must be seventy years or so. But it's been upgraded, changed, since then. The slate shingles used to be a theme around here."

"It's a wonder the state or town hasn't bought this," Justin said. "Put a little museum in here or something."

Graves snorted. "We don't need another museum around here," he said. "What in the world would we put in it? Old looms? More of that Revolutionary War junk we have all over town already?"

Justin didn't argue. He wanted the building. Though it was a few blocks from downtown, it was on the only major road going from Farmington to Albany: There was guaranteed daily traffic, people going to and from work, people driving the scenic route. It was merely a ten-minute walk from the centre of town. He believed that he understood why the place had remained empty: nobody could see the potential like he could. People in town could only see it as a factory. Still yet, being inside in the factory made him shaky—his fingers were cold, his stomach roiling. He wanted it anyway. Like how he sometimes wanted to drink whiskey, though he always woke up with a headache the next morning and could smell it in his sweat and feel it in his mouth all the next day.

He took in the room. He stood in the middle and closed his eyes. He arranged the space in his mind. He saw the coffee-shop area by the windows at the back, the wooden chairs, the salt and pepper shakers at the centre of each table. He could see the windows, clean, their shades snapped up. They looked out on the river, swollen and roaring, the sound subtly calming. The room was large, airy. He imagined a bookshelf against the back wall, filled with used books, the spines artfully tattered. He opened his eyes.

"We want this space," Justin said. "This is exactly what we had in mind."

Graves nodded. He did not appear to be excited or even convinced. He folded his hands together.

Justin spoke into the silence. "Of course, we will discuss the details later—Gary will come to meet with you, as will Phillip and David. They have the real authority to make the sale, though I can assure you that my word will convince them." Mr. Graves nodded, but Justin could not feel him give.

"Is there anything else that we need to discuss, Mr. Graves? I'd like to move forward as soon as possible." He paused. He heard his own voice in his head, the prissy formality of his sentences.

"Maybe you should see more of it before you decide," Graves said.

"What more is there to look at?"

"You should see the basement," Graves said.

"Sure," Justin said. "If you think it's a concern."

Graves turned to him. "I'm not sure if it's a concern or not. That depends," he said. "Just some people have a real reaction to the basement—it's usually a deal breaker, to tell you the truth. I don't want you to be surprised. I want you to know what you're getting."

"Sure, sure," Justin said. He followed Graves as he moved across the room, his flashlight back on.

"Not much light down here, so be careful on your way down," Graves called over his shoulder. Justin assented with a tight, silent nod. Basements were airless and contained a kind of dark that was murky even under a harsh, bare bulb. They had small slat windows high up, not large enough to let in much light or climb out of. If you were trapped, there was no second door, no windows to crawl from. No way out. He knew this. He went down anyway.

"We'll probably renovate the basement," Justin said. Speaking fixed his attention on his voice, keeping it steady and solid. "If it's just a cosmetic problem."

Graves didn't respond. He led Justin to a small door with an elaborate metal lock. He took out a crowded keychain and jiggled a long, skinny key into the door. Justin heard the little click of inner gears working and releasing.

* * *

Later, Justin would try to recall exactly what had caused him
to throw up by the passenger-side door of his car just minutes
after he and Graves emerged from the basement.

There wasn't anything obviously wrong with the basement.
It was crowded with equipment covered by tarps—lumpy,
sometimes-sharp shapes rising against the smooth, featureless
draping. A surprising amount of light filtered in through the
tiny windows. As they walked down the dark stairs, he'd felt
the sickness creeping up his throat, his stomach rioting, sweat
beading in rashes across his skin. *Jesus Christ*, he thought. *I'm
thirty-two. I'm too old to feel like this.*

It was something about the smell, he decided later. It smelled
like burning paper, like a chemical, but also something mineral,
earthy, like mounds of garden dirt. The smell was sharp and filled
the room like smoke. He had a sudden, mad thought that he
could use his hands and shape something solid in the air—that
he could reach up and cup the air and take it back to Albany with
him in a jar. The smell was also familiar. Wet dog. His mother's
hairspray. His own clothes when he hadn't washed them for days.

"It's a little musty down here," was all he said, his voice
already rasping. He brought his hand up to his throat.

Graves nodded. "The air isn't good," he said. Justin could tell
that he, too, was suffering. He cleared his throat as he led Justin
past the ghostly forms of the machines under their jackets.

"I see what you mean," Justin said, "about this part of building needing work." He imagined that if he kept speaking, the
feeling would pass.

Graves held up his hand and waved to Justin. "Come over
here," he said. "Stand right here."

Justin nodded, though the deeper he went into the room,
the sicker, more suffocated he felt.

He stood next to Graves and breathed in the silence for a few moments—not more than half a minute. And then it hit him. It wasn't a feeling, or a thought, but a sensation—a physical wave that rose up through his feet and out the top of his head like reversed lightning. He lost his vision then, his hearing—everything was muffled, fuzzy, and he could hear only a thin, piercing whine coming from somewhere inside his head, a sound like a song played back on the wrong speed setting. His thoughts spun and whistled.

Before he knew what his body was doing, he felt himself climbing, clawing really, up the basement steps, gasping for breath. He thumped his chest to loosen whatever had choked him and ran across the factory floor, through the tracks in the dust he and Graves had made, and out to his car, where he kept an emergency inhaler in the glove box.

As he released the medicine into his mouth, Graves was beside him, asking him if he was all right, if he needed to be taken to the hospital.

Justin shook his head as his throat opened. His lungs filled and he gasped.

"Just asthma," he said. "I haven't had an attack in over a year." He looked down at his hands, which shook from the sudden rush of medicine.

"It must have been the dust," he said. "The bad air in there."

Graves nodded but said nothing as Justin sat in the passenger seat, the door open, elbows on his knees and his head between his hands.

"Do you still want it?" Graves asked quietly.

Later, Justin understood that Graves had tried to warn him. He'd even shown him.

"We most certainly do," Justin said, leaning back and placing the inhaler in the glove box again, amongst old maps and registration papers and a tube of Karen's lipstick. "Like I said, we have people that can take care of things like this."

"Do you," Graves said. It was not a question, but a weary acknowledgement of Justin's illusions.

Justin nodded, though he wondered exactly who could possibly fix what was wrong with the basement. An exorcist, maybe. But he pushed those thoughts aside.

"So, if you'd like to move forward," Justin said, "I'll put you through to Gary, my supervisor, and we can start drawing up paperwork."

He dialled Gary's number, and as he did, the feeling that had been bubbling up in his stomach and throat all afternoon overwhelmed him. His fingers slipped and pushed the wrong numbers. He lips felt numb, his mouth salty.

"I'm sorry," he said. "I'm sorry." He leaned over and vomited between his shoes until his body was limp and empty of whatever sickness had temporarily possessed it.

Claire went to visit her mother in late August, after a late-night phone call in which Delia had hinted at nightmares, at wanting some comfort during the long days when Claire's father was gone doing whatever it was retired men did all day. Claire had not seen her mother since the Fourth of July, when she'd come over at her parents' bidding to eat her mother's angel food cake and watch fireworks on television, something that Claire always found strangely depressing—watching fireworks on television was like listening to an orchestra through broken headphones, like putting a pale, hotel-room landscape watercolour in a window to block the real view. But her parents had seemed to enjoy her company that night, and their strange animation had made her, in turn, less uncomfortable. Her mother had milled around her, fussing with Claire's drink and plates, whisking away knick-knacks. Delia had complained about the government, the noise from the neighbours, how quickly people drove down the road in front of the living room window.

Her father had rocked back and forth in his easy chair, the squeaking escalating as he complained about the state senator he'd seen on television arguing that Vermont should secede from the Union.

"Jesus H. Christ," he said. "What are they going to do now, the crazies we got up there? Make pot the state flower?"

Claire had laughed as her mother tsked and put her hand on Claire's shoulder.

"I don't like your father watching C-Span all the time," she said. "It's nerve wracking. All that silence and then talk talk talk and silence. They let the camera roll after everything is done and you just have to look at empty chairs and people shaking hands and leaving. It's terrible."

Her father sniffed. "I think it's peaceful."

Claire had come because she felt a different tone in her mother's voice—something eager-to-please, an attempt to keep Claire on the telephone, to make her happy. Claire was used to her mother's quick, efficient summaries, her brisk good-byes. But her latest phone call hadn't followed this pattern. She had kept Claire on the phone for almost an hour talking about nothing.

Of course Delia was lonely, Claire already knew that. She always had been. It was part of her personality, like her quick temper, her manipulation, her surprising sentimentality about holidays. But Claire had never imagined that her mother wanted her company or that her company was even preferable to loneliness.

Claire brought a bag of yarn and a crochet needle along with her. Years before, she'd asked her mother to teach her to crochet, and Delia had agreed but never followed through. Claire imagined that this was yet another example of a long list of things her mother had half-heartedly promised and then forgotten, but during the phone call, her mother mentioned crocheting again.

"Why don't you buy some beautiful dark purple yarn, honey?" she said. "We'll make something with it."

Claire was thrilled at being called *honey*. Her mother wasn't unkind, but she used terms of endearment sparingly. She was of old, Protestant Yankee stock (a fact that she was proud of—she liked to point at all the ancestors in the old graveyard who had her last name) and believed that overusing endearments cheapened them, made them meaningless.

So Claire had come with a bag of yarn and five different crochet needles—she didn't know the size she needed, or the first thing about crocheting. When she knocked on the door, she heard her mother call from somewhere deep in the house. All of the windows were open and Claire faintly heard Patsy Cline singing from Delia's clock radio, which was by her bedside, where it had been since Claire was a teenager.

I've got your picture, she's got you.

Claire opened the door. The house was as she had left it—not just since the last time she visited but since leaving for college. It hadn't changed substantially in almost fifteen years, aside from new clocks and newer versions of the same couch and chair. Claire looked down at her shoes as she removed them. After Sam's death, her parents had stripped the house bare and redecorated the cozy, lived-in, doily-dotted surfaces which had been covered with mismatched, hand-me-down furniture and family photographs in gaudy frames. Her mother had once liked soft, flowery things—the carpet had been a pale pink, the couch red-checked like a tablecloth, soft throw pillows everywhere. A year after Sam died, the entire house had changed.

"It's my allergies," Delia had explained. "I'm getting too old to spend half my day vacuuming and dusting." This wasn't true, though. Delia didn't have allergies. Sam and Claire had.

They had also changed the couch to a brown, hulking, leather loveseat that stuck to Claire's legs in the summer and was cold and crinkly against her skin in the winter. The family photos were set in simple black and silver frames and half had been taken down—all of the candid portraits were gone, leaving only the posed ones, Claire and Sam standing behind their parents, their smiles tight and unnatural.

At the time, Claire had been offended by the changes, hurt that her parents had changed things without consulting her. The thought often formed in her head, though she knew it was silly: *if Sam came back, he'd be angry that everything was different.* She imagined him coming home from school, throwing his backpack down on that cold, leather couch, and regarding the clean, metal and glass surfaces around him with horror. He had enjoyed their mother's ugly doilies, her penchant for pink and purple, with the kind of ironic fondness that young men developed toward their parents. Claire had lacked such irony—she'd sneered at her mother's acrylic yarn, her seasonal decorations, her elastic-waisted pants. Sam could afford to be amused from a distance. There was no chance that he might someday become her. Later, Claire thought that this was just another piece of evidence that Sam was a kinder, better person than her.

"Mom, where are you?" Claire called into the empty living room. She heard water beating against the enormous metal sink, deep and gleaming like the sink in an industrial kitchen. When the sink's stopper was pulled, the whoosh of water down the drain made Claire think of something ugly and misshapen crouched in the heart of a sewer—something that sucked water and meat from bones and snatched children who ventured out at night without their parents or a flashlight.

Claire entered the kitchen, blinking in a sudden, hot room full of light. Her mother had all the windows open, all the shades up. Claire lifted her hand up to her brow and made a visor. She was able to make out her mother's back, her body bent over the sink.

"I'm just finishing up the dishes," Delia called over her shoulder. She scrubbed a frying pan with a Brillo Pad, the soap foaming and spilling over her knuckles. From behind, she looked nearly half her age. From the front, though, time had not been so kind. Though her hair was scarcely streaked with grey, she had deep, long lines carved from the edges of her mouth to her chin, from eyebrows to hairline.

"Let me help you," Claire said, taking a blinding-white dishcloth (her mother soaked them in bleach weekly).

She ran the cloth over the pan and watched her mother work efficiently, savagely, on a pot crusted with macaroni and cheese.

"I brought the yarn."

"What?" Delia didn't look up from her work.

"The yarn," Claire said. "You said you wanted to teach me to crochet."

Delia pressed her lips together and scrubbed harder. Her knuckles knocked against the pan as she scrubbed.

"Of course," she said. "After the dishes."

Claire nodded and took the wet pan from her mother's hands. She wiped each dish and pot and pan completely dry. When they finished, Claire hoped, as she often had as a teenager, as a college student returning temporarily to a place she no longer understood or belonged, that her mother had noticed how obedient she was, how well she had completed the small task given to her. But she only asked Claire to go in the living room and wait while she made some tea.

Claire sat in the living room as Delia moved around in the kitchen, clicking cups, running the sink. Claire could hear the soft, foamy sound of boiling water being poured into cups of her mother's always faintly stale and tasteless tea. Her mother drank her tea with heaping teaspoons of sugar and a quarter cup of milk, so she probably never noticed the difference. Claire drank hers straight, as she did her coffee and her liquor on the rare occasions when she went out to drink or bought a glass of something clear and fiery to help sleep or calm her nerves.

Delia entered the room, staring down at the tea in her hands, the cup's delicate handles tight around her swollen knuckles. She hissed as water splashed on her hand. Claire rose to her feet and eased the cup from her.

"Thank you," Claire said, blowing on the hot water as steam billowed from it. She smiled. She wanted to put her mother at ease—even here in her own living room, Delia's eyes were darting, distracted, as she sucked on the skin between her thumb and forefinger, where she'd been splashed.

"I'm sorry my tea burned you," Claire said.

"Don't be silly. You didn't have anything to do with it being hot or burning me." Delia set down her teacup after taking a tiny, experimental sip. She sniffled, rubbed her hand under her nose, and looked away.

She was crying, Claire realized. *Oh Christ*, she thought. *They're getting a divorce. Mom has cancer. Dad has cancer.* Almost immediately, at the thought of hospitals, of treatments, she remembered Sam's funeral, which had taken place on an ungodly beautiful day in September, a day bright and colourful as a postcard from the corner store. She thought of Sam in the coffin, his skin white and pasty, the colour painted on garishly, inexpertly, making him look like a doll of a boy. She couldn't do it again, not yet. She needed more time.

"What's wrong?" Claire asked.

Her mother shook her head and covered her eyes with her fists. She rubbed the tears away, her mascara smearing into the crepey skin around her eyes.

Claire had never seen her mother cry over nothing before. She'd cried when she broke her collarbone a few years earlier— she slid on a patch of ice in front of the house on Christmas Eve and crashed down with an audible *snap*. But she didn't cry about anything less serious than a broken bone, at least not in front of people.

Her mother plucked a tissue from her sleeve, where she kept them gathered like magician's scarves, and wiped under her eyes.

"I'm sorry," she said. "I'm sorry to get worked up like that."

"It's okay," Claire said. "What's wrong?"

Delia looked out the living room window. Claire followed her gaze. She looked out to the lawn, green as algae, the clear sky above it. Children roamed the sidewalks in packs or alone, texting or listening to their earbuds. She felt a sudden, painful desire to be the Claire of twenty years ago—too bored to even turn on the television, too hot and listless to get up and go outside or go up to her room and read. Then, everything was coming later, and she was only waiting for it. Waiting for Sam, for somebody she knew to pass, for somebody to see her and say hello and offer her something interesting to see and do.

"Did you hear what they are going to do with the factory?" her mother asked suddenly. "How they're going to put a store in there, some coffee shop?" She shook her head. "It's a shame the town would let it happen."

Claire looked at her mother. It hadn't even occurred to her that she might be upset about the factory. Claire had already drafted a letter of protest to send to the newspaper, to the Beans company headquarters, and personally to this Justin Hemmings, who was overseeing the design and staffing at this new location, but she didn't expect much to come of it. She'd lived in Farmington her entire life, so she knew how things worked. The people in charge had already made their decisions.

"I did hear." Claire pressed her hands against her knees. She didn't want to cry in front of her mother. "I'm going to send a letter to the paper," she said.

"Please don't send a letter to the paper." Delia said, shaking her head, pressing her lips together in a sour pucker. "We don't need everyone to know our business."

Claire sighed. "How else can we protest," she said, "if nobody knows we are upset?"

Her mother busied herself with putting heaps of sugar into her tea. "Why don't you talk to Miriam Hastings?" she said. "You know, up at the municipal building? I bet she would be willing to cause a stir if she knew how we felt. I bet she would have something to say about it."

Miriam Hastings, the Assistant Town Manager, was the right-hand woman of Town Manager Dick Stevens, a former police chief with a fierce, often angry face that made him seem perpetually aggravated. It was his eyebrows, Claire had decided. She wondered if he had gotten most of his promotions based solely on the authority in those eyebrows.

Miriam Hastings was another story. She was the soft face of Farmington—the person you could appeal to if you wanted to have a Humane Society benefit at the town gazebo or a cancer research barbecue on the church lawn. Claire had written several letters to Miriam when the library went through a sharp funding cut in the early aughts. She'd asked for the town to contribute to keep the afternoon teen reading groups going. Miriam was the accessible side of the town, though she was known for being sharp, even a little harsh, with those she didn't like or respect.

"What does Miriam Hastings have to do with the factory?" Claire asked. She assumed private business didn't need much from town officials.

Her mother poured milk into her cup, turning the tea to a cloudy muck.

"She lost a family member in that factory, too." She looked up and met Claire's eyes. "Miriam's one of us."

One of us. Claire let that go. "What do you mean? Who did she lose?"

As far as Claire could tell, Miriam and her family were golden, untouched by tragedy of even the smallest kind—a lost dog, one profligate child. Miriam was in her mid-sixties at least, but could pass for a woman in her early fifties. Her three children were attractive and academically successful. Her husband had been a dentist in the area before his retirement. Claire didn't associate Miriam Hastings with death.

"Her aunt was one of the women killed in the factory."

Claire knew about the fire. Claire remembered her teacher discussing it on Town Heritage day, when her entire fourth-grade class spent a day walking from green-streaked plaque to statue to monument, trekking all across Farmington until the school bus loaded them up, exhausted, and took them to Friendly's for ice cream. They had visited the catamount statue in Old Farmington; the cat's muscles bulged around its elbows and shoulders, its teeth pulled back in a snarl. Jenny, a particularly lovely and malicious blonde with perfectly symmetrical pig-tails, had told Claire that catamounts still prowled around Old Farmington and that she should be careful. Claire hadn't believed it, but large, powerful cats had since occupied her nightmares. They'd visited the small stone monument by the old battleground celebrating the capture of an enemy weapons cache during the Revolutionary War. Claire had learned the word *cache* that day, a word that sounded exactly like what it was: a hidden place. And they had walked to the factories, already largely abandoned, already part of history.

Back then, the factory hadn't meant much to her. She and Sam had been in the same class.

They listened as their teacher, Mrs. Salsburg, in her usual polyester slacks and gauzy shirt (sometimes so gauzy that Claire thought she could see a whisper of Mrs. Salsburg's bra, a scandalous sight), told them about the proud history of textiles in Farmington. She explained that the waterwheel, which was still turning behind the factory, had once powered all of the machines. She then told them about the fire that had almost destroyed it in the fifties, how the owners had rebuilt it so that it looked almost exactly as it had before.

The factory had made her uneasy, even then. Maybe it had something to do with the quality of light—by then, the sky had darkened and it had grown colder. She remembered taking Sam's hand as they trudged behind Mrs. Salsburg to see the waterwheel. The water was loud and furious that day, the river swollen and rushing around the wheel, the slats violently catching the waves and flinging them up as it cut through the river. The water was muddy and churned milk chocolate-coloured foam at its edges. Mrs. Salsburg, sensing imminent rain, called them back to the sidewalk, where they walked back to their bus parked near the town plaza. They got to Friendly's just in time to see the first raindrops, the first shivers of lightning illuminating the clouds from behind like lights behind the angel hair on a Christmas tree. Claire and Sam had walked home after school under the same umbrella, exhausted after all of the walking but nervous from the sudden influx of sugar—they rarely ever ate desserts at home and felt energized by the double-dip mint chocolate-chip ice cream cones they had both chosen. They kicked in the puddles and talked about the places in town they had liked the most. Sam had liked the catamount statue because it looked real, as if it could come to life and jump down and eat anyone who teased it. Claire had liked the plaza and the gazebo, where Old Sammy, their own Revolutionary War hero (he had gathered a unit of farmers to hold off the British—though the British had never arrived, a fact conveniently left off the plaques), had made a speech to the people of the town about standing up for their country, for their people, in the midst of fear and chaos and threats from *The King*. Claire knew that *The King* meant England, the whole thing, not just the King, but she liked to imagine a letter from the King himself, arriving in an enormous, gold-embossed envelope, personally threatening Farmington's freedom.

They had both agreed that the factory was the creepiest part of town—even creepier than the deer park, where deer with patchy fur, the pink of their skin showing where they'd rubbed it away, nibbled at the edges of the fence and slept among the weeds and tall grass.

Claire's mother had told her not to believe in ghosts. "Those are just stories to scare girls and boys," she'd said, and Claire didn't want to be just another girl or boy. Sam had agreed. "No ghosts," he said. "Only Heaven or Hell, like in the Bible." She and Sam had sometimes gone to Sunday school at St. Mary's Church. Their parents encouraged them to go, though they didn't seem particularly interested in what Claire and Sam had learned in class. Claire suspected they just wanted a morning to themselves to drink coffee and read the Sunday paper in peace. Still, the lesson about Hell had impressed them both, and for a while they tried very hard to please God, until the summer, when they forgot about fire and the gnashing of teeth and stayed out past dark and went to the river, though they weren't supposed to, and sometimes stole packs of gum from the gas station.

By the time Claire had left her mother's house, she had agreed to meet with Miriam Hastings about the factory.

"You have to go out on a limb," her mother had said. Her tears had left a slight delicacy around her eyes, a pinkness that reminded Claire of the nervous eyes of white rabbits.

"You *should* want to stand up for your brother," she said.

Claire could not argue with this. She should want to stand up for her brother. She agreed that she would try to arrange a meeting with Miriam. After drinking her tea, she said that she was exhausted, that she had to get home. Her mother agreed that it was getting late, that she should probably finish with her cleaning, though Claire could see no evidence that there was anything left to be cleaned—the entire house smelled of lemons and the chalky acid of Ajax.

Her mother had never gotten around to teaching her how to crochet. Claire balled up her yarn and needles in a plastic bag and carried them back to her apartment. She felt that her mother was punishing her in a new and impossible-to-complain-about way.

She reached her apartment just before seven thirty, as the light began to dim. It was almost cool that August night, and Claire knew that fall would be coming soon. September was her worst month. The therapist she'd seen for many years once noted that all of her major depressions had occurred in September. Of course, it was the anniversary of Sam's death—it didn't take a therapist to point that out. But his death, and her feelings around it, had seeped into everything else about September—leaves dying brightly, falling and catching the light, the blue skies, the cinnamon smell of the branches and dirt drying up, curling away to prepare for winter. When she looked out the window in September, she sometimes thought it would be different, that it wouldn't be the same that year, but it always was the same, especially on the golden days.

The night he'd died had been warm, beautiful and clear. As she'd run home, the memory of Sam's gurgling, wet breathing still on her mind, she had picked a red leaf from her hair. It had tangled in her ponytail and tickled against her ear as she ran.

That night she took out a bottle of red wine she'd bought from the corner store. She didn't know much about wine, but she knew that she liked the dry, acid wines, the kind that made her tongue feel like it had been stung. She drank glass after glass in the low light of her kitchen. Her cat cried and whipped around her ankles, asking for food or attention. She watched the black square of her kitchen window, perfectly blank above the confusion of dirty cups and plates and saucers in her sink, and tried to think of what she could possibly say to convince Miriam Hastings, Assistant Town Manager, to discourage the addition of at least twenty-five new jobs in Farmington.

When Justin returned home, he told Karen nothing about what he had experienced at the factory—at least nothing of what had happened to him. He told her that the visit had gone well, that they would take the building. She had not smiled at the news. She had not congratulated him.

"So, we might be moving," she said.

"I don't know. We'll have to talk about it," he said.

She didn't reply.

"I'm feeling a bit sick from all of the driving," he said. "I'm going to go up to bed early." She didn't argue with him.

That night, after swallowing a sleeping pill with a glass of wine, Justin dreamed of the factory. His dreams were vivid and ugly, and he felt a sharp pain in his ribs, though he could not remember how the pain had gotten there or any other details.

In the morning, he woke exhausted, his muscles spent and faintly tender.

He called Gary to report that the factory was exactly what they were looking for.

By the time he hung up, Justin was no longer troubled by the dream. He no longer had the stale smell in his nose, the ache in his muscles. He was triumphant. He would move the company forward. He would create something beautiful and lasting. His life would be there, in that peaceful town. And it would be a real life, not the makeshift, temporary thing he had with Karen in this rented apartment, in this small city he felt no allegiance to, in this place that had never felt like home, no matter how long he had lived there. He would love where he lived and where he worked. Not many people could say that.

His father had worked at a bread factory, a flat, completely utilitarian building at the edge of a river. It had been built in the fifties, during the craze for things like Tupperware, manufactured homes, and televisions dinners. It was made of squares within squares within squares, the inside walls cream-coloured, the parking lot an expanse of concrete broken only with yellow lines. Sometimes, when Justin's mother would pick his father up from work, Justin would wait for him in the parking lot, watching as workers emerged from the doors at five thirty, watching for his father to appear in the crowd of almost identical men— all dressed in blue work shirts with their names embroidered on the pockets, tan slacks, and black shoes. He knew his father because he dragged his left foot slightly—it was an almost imperceptible limp, but his father referenced it almost daily. His lame foot had kept him out of the Navy, had made him a laughingstock at school, had caused him to drop out in tenth grade, had made him unable to do manual labour, had stuck him in factories doing *women's work* (though mostly men worked at the factory, a detail Justin never pointed out when his father was on one of his tirades), work that he feared was making him soft. Justin began to regard the foot as his father did—a terrible blight on his father's life, the thing that had caused them to live in a rented house with leaking ceilings, two children per room, a nagging wife, all of it a result of that slightly weak, slightly dragging foot. Justin knew that he was part of that unwanted life, an appendage like the foot, only worse because he needed to be fed and cared for. He tried to make himself small and quiet to ease his father's bitterness. He spoke in a whisper. He ate very little.

Justin remembered, when he was as young as eight or nine, sitting up at night and planning his future. He decided that he

would take up a paper route. Lots of kids did it in the summer. He imagined himself awake in the dark of early morning, slinging a pack full of papers across his back, wheeling his
bike with the rusty chain from the garage, and setting out by
himself in the strange, orange light of early morning, a time
when only farm trucks and semi-truck drivers were out. The
idea of being awake that early, when almost everybody else was
in bed and dreaming, was an obsession. It was a kind of power,
being awake when everyone else was asleep. It was appealing,
too, having a job of his own, money in his pocket that he had
earned.

Farmington made him think of Clark's River, his hometown. Farmington was much more upscale, with that small,
liberal arts college with its vast, perfectly landscaped yard and
surrounding stone wall. But it had its history, too. Its east side
looked like Clark's River, with its rows of empty factories and
old factory houses, now chopped up into multi-family apartment housing, the air conditioners sagging from the windows,
play kitchens and grubby plastic tricycles poking out from the
overgrown weeds on the lawn. He knew Farmington, and he
knew what it needed—it needed an injection of success.

Sometimes, while at a business meeting or at lunch with
a colleague, Justin would look down at his lunch, at his water
bubbling in its glass, at the buttons on his jacket, and wonder if
people could tell that he didn't really belong there, that he had
grown up in a house with holes in the walls and been picked on
at school for only taking a bath once a week. But now, nobody
knew who he really was. He looked like everyone else. And he
would breathe easier, begin to listen again to whatever his boss
was saying with PowerPoint, to whatever his office friend was
talking about over their fifteen-dollar salads.

He often dreamed of Clark's River. He dreamed that he woke
in his old bed, his sister snoring. It was early, the thin, pink light

of five in the morning, just like in his fantasies about the paper route. But he was an adult in his old bed again, holding his knees in the cold. He wanted to get up and look around. What would he find in the drawers in the kitchen, in the bathroom cupboards? Would his mother be awake in the kitchen, her hair still coiled and pinned up in tight rollers? Would his father be alive again, sipping milk and waiting for his Advil to kick in? Justin pushed the blankets aside and put his bare feet on the floor. It was cold, so cold that he felt, even within the dream, that he was awake, that he was aware, and that he wasn't a child again. Then he heard it. At first he couldn't tell what it was, a strange scrape and bump, like somebody dragging a body over concrete. Then, he remembered. It was his father coming to get him out of bed, to get him up and ready for school, to get him to go feed the dogs or scrape the ice from the windshield or help his mother with breakfast. As he heard the steps getting closer, Justin pulled his feet from the floor and pressed his knees to his chest again. *Thump, slide, thump.* He was an adult. And he was lost here, shivering in bed, his dead father coming to wake him.

Justin would wake in the warm blankets in his own room. His younger sister was sleeping somewhere in her own bed in upstate New York, her husband beside her, her four children in their beds. His brothers lived in various places in Upstate New York, all safe as far as he knew. And knowing all of this, he would be grateful that he couldn't go back, that he couldn't be trapped, and that time went only forward and never back.

II

NOVEMBER 17TH, 1957

Joan had worked at the dress factory for five years—since just after her senior year in high school, when she'd been a skinny girl who favoured high, tight ponytails, her blue eyes rimmed by dark lashes. She looked at old photographs, the ones in the yearbook where she was posing at the top of the cheerleading triangle or singing in the choir, and she couldn't remember a single time when she had not been loved. She wished she could remember being that girl.

It wasn't that millwork was particularly hard. It had simply made her an adult. Now she wore heels and dresses. She cut her hair fashionably short and set it every night in rollers. She wore the matte red lipstick of women in magazines. She was an adult. She was beautiful, like women in the movies who clicked their heels and smarted off to the men who flirted with them and snapped their compacts closed. Like those women, she'd leave the town she came from, though the women in movies always came from somewhere in the Midwest, with farm boys back home who pined for them. Leaving Farmington would be easy: nobody was pining for her. She'd come back for Christmas, of course, to go to Mass with her parents and see the piles of white lilies and listen to the songs about God and Jesus and Mary swell and overwhelm the church, filling the big, empty place with their insistent repetitions about love and miracles. She would open presents and eat her mother's molasses-soaked fruitcakes, the candied cherries sticking in her molars, making her teeth hurt. But she would not live here.

Since she was only temporary, she could enjoy walking to the factory, wearing her apron and pulling her hair back, collecting her cheque and putting the money under her mattress. It was a lark. It was almost like acting: she would get up in the morning and dress herself as though she was going onto a movie set.

Her mother sometimes called her conceited, said she thought she was *above the company*. And though Joan knew pride was a sin, she couldn't help it—she thought she *was* above the company, usually. The company bored her stiff and the idea of spending her life like them made her want to do something truly scandalous, like take a train to Boston and become a lounge singer, or live a bohemian life in New York City, where she'd wear trousers and black turtlenecks and smoke marijuana. She'd heard about women like that in magazines and they always came to bad ends, pregnant or scorned by fast men, their names ruined. But those were just stories. She thought it might be different in real life.

Joan walked to the mill from her parents' house in Old Farmington, where she kept her girlhood room in the attic, a room she had begged for at the age of twelve. The room was cramped and slope-ceilinged and always too hot or too cold, but she loved it. It was her own prayer closet (though she did not pray), her secret room. In the summer, she opened her small window, unbuttoned her shirt, and sprawled out on the floor and read magazines in the almost altogether, the wind cooling her back. In the winter, she wore two pairs of socks and wrapped herself in a quilt and read. It was enough to be alone, separate from the house downstairs that clattered and hummed with ugly, voiceless energy.

Her parents wanted better for her, they said. They had wanted her to marry a fellow Catholic and have grandchildren for them, just as her sister Patricia had, as her brothers Arthur and John had. The boys both lived in New York and came only for holidays, their smiling wives in demure coral lipstick, hair stiff from monthly permanents. Her brothers made their money doing things that made Joan too bored to even remember, things with numbers and pieces of carbon paper. They had secretaries and meetings.

Patricia, Joan's older sister, still lived in Farmington. She was tall and gaunt, and her children clung to her like briers. When she and the children came to visit—all four of them under ten and therefore almost impossible for Joan to talk to—the house warbled like an aviary with their restless, directionless energy. Patricia sighed, screamed at the children, and smiled tightly at any questions about her life. "We are fine," she always said. "Just busy. Just living our everyday life." She said the words *everyday life* as though describing something necessary but completely miserable, like a dental appointment. She talked to Joan as if Joan didn't have an everyday life.

"We don't need things to be new," she'd say, smiling her unhappy smile. "Not all of us have to be entertained all the time," she added.

Patricia often asked Joan when she was going to complete her duties as a woman and find a husband and have children. "You aren't getting any younger," she would say.

Joan had no desire to complete her duties as a woman if those duties made her as unhappy as her mother and sister seemed, but she needed them, for now, and was grateful that her mother let her live at home, though she knew that she was a kind of burden—proof that the parenting and care they had lavished on her had not been enough to make her a good, faithful Catholic woman.

Joan did not love the church, as she knew she should. She didn't believe that the fat man in a toupee at the front of the congregation, in his heavy, curtain-drab robes, had any closer connection to God than she did. She saw how the priest looked when he placed the wafer on her tongue, the wine glass against her lips. He liked the power, and he liked to put his hands in places that most women wouldn't allow a strange man to touch. He lingered when he laid the bread on her tongue. He sometimes touched her chin when he tipped the glass. She knew enough about life to know what his looks meant. She didn't mistake them for the love of God.

But she didn't blame him either—*best to get pleasure where you can*, she thought.

Joan wanted to be a writer. She didn't know quite what she wanted to write yet—maybe plays, or movie scripts, or shows for television. She scribbled ideas in a notebook her mother had given her a year earlier for Christmas—a leather-bound thing that shut with a cheap tin lock.

She had hundreds of plots and character sketches. She had started the dialogue for some of them, scenes that moved quickly, wittily—at least she hoped—but she never felt free to complete them. Just when she felt that she might be ready to write more, to finish a whole scene, when she had her pen poised above her spiral-bound notebook, she'd hear a creak or a crash from below: her mother moving furniture, cleaning, washing dishes, crashing the pans together to make it clear that at least *she* was working, even if nobody else was. The urge to write left as soon as Joan heard Betty's fretful movements. Her parents were down there, disappointed in her, wishing that she were a different person, wishing that she wasn't still there, in the bedroom where she used to study for spelling tests and have slumber parties.

Joan spent her days after work scribbling as best she could, and her nights reading the big leather-bound novels she got from the library—the Brontë sisters, Dickens, and gothic romances, mostly. Reading about little Jane Eyre, locked up inside herself for so many years, finally free at the end, finally mistress of her own house and husband and desires, made Joan think of herself in her attic. She wasn't quiet and she wasn't plain but she was trapped and had to go through the motions until she could be free. But she would get away when the time was right. Everything happened when the time was right.

She sometimes went to the movies by herself or with a girl-friend—somebody who didn't pop her gum during the movie or insist on buying a package of loud candy. She would sink down in her seat, allowing the sounds to fill her, allowing the colours to overwhelm any thoughts that might be trying to crawl up and distract her from the blonde in a pink dress running across a cornfield, from the man in a blue suit pacing his office, smoke billowing from his nostrils and mouth.

Joan had almost ended up like her sister. Just a few years before, she'd stood crying for joy in front of her high school sweetheart Richard Wallis' house after she'd missed her period for three weeks straight the summer after senior year. Then, she had wanted, more than anything, to have her life fixed for good, to have her days made clear and coherent and filled with duty and purpose. You couldn't make the wrong choice if you had a family, a husband, a little house—it was right, and everyone thought so. Just keeping a house running was some kind of miracle, according to most people, something a woman was specially made to do. So Joan had let him pull her skirt up in the car after they had gone to see some movie with Lauren Bacall and Humphrey Bogart—she couldn't remember much of the movie, but something about it had made Richard turn and press his wet, moving mouth against hers. She had gone through with it because she wanted to be a good sport, and she thought maybe this meant that Richard loved her enough, and maybe, if he married her, she'd finally be able to leave home.

Instead of embracing her and offering marriage on the spot, Richard had given her money to go see a doctor in Albany famous for his discretion, to make sure she was *in a condition*. Joan had gone with Richard on the pretence that they were going on a date in Albany to see the new Fred Astaire film. As she entered the examination area, a white, antiseptic little room without even a droopy watercolour of foliage to break the monotony, she wished desperately that she really were going to see a film full of lurid colours and dance numbers.

She put her feet in the cold stirrups and flinched when the doctor snapped on his gloves, tensed when she felt the pressure of his fingers.

"I've never done this before," Joan said, hoping he would soothe her. She was shocked that a man her father's age was looking at places she never let anyone look. She had imagined that she'd be dressed in a white robe and that everything would be done by X-ray machine. She hadn't imagined his hands, or the cold metal, or the pinch and stretch of her skin. Her forehead perspired.

"Don't tense," he said. "Please relax."

She tried to relax by closing her eyes and thinking of her attic room—how warm it was, how when she got home the first thing she'd do was bring a big glass of Coke up to her room and sip it slowly as she read a book.

Soon, after a few pinches, the doctor told her to slide back up, unlace her feet from the stirrups, and put her clothes back on. He left the room abruptly and she hurried to dress, unsure of when he would return.

The doctor, who even looked like Joan's father, with his bushy brows and a tired, heavily lined mouth, said there was nothing wrong with her besides a little nervousness, which sometimes caused *women's troubles and delays in the natural cycles.* He told her that she would have her *monthly visit* as soon as she stopped worrying so much and calmed down. He gave her some pills in an orange bottle, each as big as the multivitamins her mother took every morning with her orange juice. He didn't say what they did, just to take them at night if she had trouble sleeping or felt particularly nervous. She shook the bottle and the pills thunked heavily against the glass.

Joan left the office red-faced. She wanted to take a long, scalding bath. She wanted to be by herself. She picked up a movie magazine in the lobby as she waited for Richard to return in his father's black car.

As she waited, she read an article about Joan Crawford, who had saved up money on her own to go to drama school, then ran off to Hollywood to make herself famous. Joan liked sharing a name with this woman in heavy shoulder pads, her eyebrows thick, hair glossy. The article was accompanied by a full-page spread of Crawford in a bathing suit, reclined on a one-armed divan, her red lips and black hair like ink against the creamy upholstery. She was almost forty and still beautiful. She thought about Joan Crawford riding the bus from the Midwest to Hollywood alone and recalled the doctor resting his gloved hands on her thighs, applying metal to her thinnest skin. Joan Crawford wouldn't let herself be embarrassed by such a thing.

She was free now, just like Joan Crawford. She wasn't bound to anyone or anything anymore—the doctor had said that everything was normal. No baby. And she was lucky to be free, to have her body all to herself, to not have to marry Richard, whom she wasn't sure she liked all that much anyway. She'd never really thought about it before. She'd only known that he liked her, and that had seemed like enough. She looked up from the magazine, Joan Crawford's face flattening and darkening as the glare moved across the page. She looked around the empty waiting room. She almost wished for somebody to tell about her good fortune, her freedom, but there was nobody. Richard would be coming any minute. She put down the magazine and closed her eyes. She was alone.

Richard slowly drifted out of her life after that day. She did not cut things off abruptly—she was too used to his company, too afraid of hurting him—but gradually she grew colder to his embraces. As he talked about baseball, about how he wanted to be on the Farmington Town Select Board like his father and grandfather had been, and described the kind of life he wanted—quiet, happy, filled with soft chairs and shag carpet and a camping trip every once in a while, nothing too rugged, maybe a pop-up trailer at the local National Park every summer—Joan grew more and more certain that she had to let him go. He was a sweet, kind, perfectly normal boy, and he bored her. He was no longer the only way out of her parents' house. She began to see the things about him that her mind had skimmed over before—he picked his teeth after dinner, he spit on the sidewalk, he only liked to watch movies that were funny or about war. She couldn't remember saying anything definitive. She could only remember his presence, and then his gradual absence. That, too, brought relief.

Joan decided soon after that she would work until she'd saved up enough money to live wherever she wanted to live and do whatever she wanted to do. She figured she'd need at least a few hundred to take the bus to her next home, wherever it was, to get an apartment, to feed herself until she found a job. She gave herself three years at the most. By then, if she didn't have enough money, she'd go anyway—she'd have a whole five years of work experience, so she wouldn't be in such bad shape. She didn't know where she wanted to go—maybe Boston, maybe New York City, maybe even Montréal. She'd had three years of French in school and a Berlitz book that she practised with every night before bed. She could make it wherever she decided to go.

She applied for a sewing position at the New England Textiles factory, just a few blocks away from her parents' house.

Joan got a sewing position, kept her girlhood room, and saved her money under her mattress. She gave her mother ten dollars a month to help with expenses. Betty always shook her head and pursed her lips, as though Joan were presenting her with a pack of pornographic cards instead of money. But Betty always took the money and bought lavish Sunday dinners that Joan ate heartily, gratefully. Joan thought she should savour those meals, that someday they would be a sweet, distant memory.

On November 17th, Joan walked slowly to work; she'd be leaving soon, there was no point in hurrying. It was beautiful outside, the sun warm against her wool jacket. She listened to the click of her shoes against the pavement and watched the last, yellow leaves detach in the wind, swirling down and collecting where the street met the jut of sidewalk.

Today, Joan was going to give her two weeks' notice to Tony, the foreman at New England Textiles. Tony had been the boss for the last two years. He was no trouble. Just a gross, brutish man—he smelled like oil and perfume, his hair always slick, his suits food-spotted and sloppy, hanging from his thin body like rags from a scarecrow. But he was relatively quiet (not a chatterbox, a quality Joan couldn't stand in men or women) and content to let everyone do their job as they had before he arrived. He wasn't poor, Joan was sure, but he dressed as though he got all of his clothes out of the Saint Mary's consignment shop.

"I'm not here to change anything on you ladies," Tony said on his first day, when he gathered all the women together to introduce himself.

He flashed a grin and Joan noticed that his teeth were perfectly formed and white.

Tony had made mild overtures of affection toward her. Once he placed his hand on her shoulder when she happened to be out back smoking on her lunch break, eating a tuna fish sandwich while watching the river flow angrily over the boulders and rocks that choked it. She'd been watching the foam gather in furious little explosions when she suddenly felt pressure on her shoulder. She turned, frightened, almost dropping her sandwich. But it was only Tony. She had been thinking of the river, how it was going fast enough for somebody to drown in it, and she had a sudden vision of him picking her up and pitching her into it.

"I'm glad somebody else is out here," he said. "I hate to stand around and smoke alone." He shook a cigarette loose from the pack bulging his shirt pocket. He had taken off his usual droopy sports jacket. His dress shirt was the colour of old bone. Yellow stains crept up the collar and cuffs.

"You interested in having dinner with me sometime?" he asked abruptly. He squinted, bared his teeth. He had probably meant to prepare with some small talk, to try and charm her. Joan felt for him—it was hard to say the right thing at the right time.

Despite her sympathy, Joan moved away, her face twitching, lips turning with something like distaste, like when she got a mouthful of bad milk. His hand fell back to his side. He removed the cigarette from his mouth, blew smoke in the space between them. He looked down at his shoes. She had embarrassed him.

Joan remembered her job, her savings, her plans for leaving. She forced a smile.

"That's a nice offer," she said. "But I have a boyfriend."

She didn't have a boyfriend, but she didn't want Tony to think he had a chance. Joan had heard that he'd come on to a few of the other girls, too. It was harmless, though. She'd come across many men like this at the local bars—men approaching or just over forty who were surprised to find themselves bachelors, eager to bag a young, sweet wife, to start late on that life they had seen other people live for so many years.

"It's a shame a girl like you gets herself tied down so young," he said.

She smiled in response and finished her cigarette. She threw the smouldering butt down to the ground and rubbed it out with the toe of her pump.

"I'm just the kind of girl who likes to settle down, I guess."

Since then, she hadn't had much trouble from him. A few unnecessary touches as he passed her on the way out the door— nothing that she couldn't handle. Nothing that everybody else under thirty didn't get.

Joan continued her walk to work, picking up the pace as the bells at St. Mary's tolled nine o'clock.

Joan checked the threading on her machine, ran a practice stitch across a piece of fabric, and began her day's work. She smiled as she ran a long, even line up the bodice of a dress, which was covered in a sickly, paisley pattern of tan and pale pink.

After two weeks, she would never have to see these paisley shirtdresses again. She wanted to stand up and throw the dress on the floor and invite everyone to trample on it in celebration. But she kept sewing.

* * *

Tony went down to the basement, banging his keys against his thigh. He was going to meet Charlotte, the little redhead in the dyeing room. He had first noticed how cute she was, how sweetly her small body fit her skirts and plain, white shirts when he passed her during work about three months ago. He'd taken her out to dinner soon after and learned she was just out of high school but practically living on her own with only a roommate she never saw to keep track of her. None of the girls seemed to know her well; she was from out of town, maybe a farm girl. It was better that way—less gossip.

He asked her about herself on the first date, which made her blush. *There's nothing important about me,* she'd told him, fluttering her false eyelashes in a gesture of shyness—genuine, not the usual imitation shyness Tony saw in most girls her age. He liked to know exactly where his girlfriends were from. He was sympathetic to girls who were from the country, who said *shears* instead of *scissors* and wore the wrong kinds of shoes and stockings. It was easier to teach them. They didn't have ideas about how much they knew already.

He found Charlotte crouched unsteadily on her heels, hampered by her tight skirt. She warmed her hands by the kerosene heater at her feet. Tony had placed them all around the factory, including here in the basement, where the walls were surrounded by black, cold dirt. *Cold as a coffin*, he sometimes thought when he was down there counting inventory.

A can of kerosene, its cap undone, filled the room with a sharp, dizzying smell.

"Jesus, Charlotte, shut the kerosene." He shouted more loudly than he had intended. It scared him, an image of Charlotte lying on the basement floor, her mouth and eyes open, poisoned by fumes.

Charlotte looked up at his outburst—he didn't usually shout at her but spoke to her as one would a particularly impressionable child. She made a surprised "O" with her mouth. Her face was puffy from crying, with black, thick eye makeup streaked down her cheeks.

"What's wrong?" Tony asked. He put the keys in his pocket and went to her, kneeling into the warmth of the heater. "Did something happen?"

Charlotte sniffled and mumbled, her breath hitching. He shuffled forward and pressed her face against his chest, patted her head. The heater blew against the fabric of his shirt, making an uncomfortable hot spot on his back. He could smell the polyester heating, a smell like when he left a plastic lid on a burner.

He didn't like to see women upset, and particularly Charlotte, who seemed more like a bright child than a grown woman. She made him think of his sister, Shelly, who had stayed behind in Poultney and married a boy who worked on the roads, a boy who'd beaten her in the beginning, before Tony told him that he'd snap his neck if Shelly had as much as a red cheek. She was prone to crying, to hysterics, and to collapsing in a heap when something was the matter. She had a softness about her eyes and mouth that made her seem impressionable. That, Tony had to admit, made the idea of hitting her seem sometimes attractive even to him, and he loved his sister.

Charlotte, too, had a funny softness around her eyes and mouth. If you pressed your fingers into her skin, their impression might remain there for a long while.

Charlotte raised her head, sniffling. She rubbed her eyes, spreading a swatch of black makeup across her temple.

"I have something to tell you, Tony." She sniffled again, staring at her smudged hands.

She wasn't just upset—she was a mess. Her hair was dull and limp, and her jumper had a stain, egg yolk or mustard, over the right breast. She'd probably slept in yesterday's clothes.

"I went to the doctor," she said, her breath rising. "I was late with, you know, *my friend*. I'm going to have a baby."

Tony watched her sit and sob, her body quaking. He wobbled slightly at the sound of her crying, the smell of the kerosene, and the damned bad luck of what she'd told him. His stomach quivered at the edge of sickness—he could taste the greasy ghost of his breakfast, bacon and eggs, at the back of his throat.

Being in the basement didn't help. It made him queasy to be down there for long. There was something ugly about the air—the lack of circulation, the smell of rot.

"Just let yourself cry," Tony said. "Just cry it out and then we'll talk."

Charlotte wiped away her tears with the cuff of her shirt and Tony paced the room. So she was going to have a baby. Something would have to be done. He felt in his pocket for the keys. He would need to lock the door before somebody heard her crying and came down. Then he wouldn't be able to stop the talking. They've probably already heard. Tony imagined a gaggle of women outside the door, waiting to hear what he would say next.

"We're going to sit down and talk about this, Charlotte," he said. She looked as though she might begin to cry again at his words. Tony went to her.

"Now, I think you know the situation." He assumed his voice of authority and reason. He stopped rooting for his keys and crouched down, looked her in the eye. *Now is the time to comfort*, he thought. *She'll stop crying and we'll go out to dinner tonight and she'll brush her hair and paint her nails and we can get out of this god-awful box that stinks of kerosene and dirt.*

"I'm going to give you enough cash to get this fixed, okay?" Tony pushed lightly against her shoulder with his fingertips. She looked up at him, but her face was absolutely still, composed, and unreadable.

"I won't leave you alone with this problem—I'm going to help you get rid of it." Tony stood up, his knees popping with the effort. "But let me get the door first—we don't want anyone barging in on us." Tony hooked his key ring with his index finger and walked toward the door. He didn't look behind to see that Charlotte had risen, too. She grasped his elbow, nearly jerked him off his feet.

"No," she said quietly, but firmly, in a voice that seemed impossibly calm and assured for a woman who just a moment ago hadn't been able to string more than two words together. "I'm keeping it," she said. "You don't have to marry me, but I'm keeping it."

She had hold of his arm at the elbow. Her red, almond-shaped nails dug into his skin.

"Do you hear me?" she said. "I could never get rid of it. That would be a sin. I can go away. I can live somewhere else. I can leave here and all you have to do is send me a little money sometimes. You don't even have to visit. You don't have to have anything to do with me if you don't want to. I'll just need a little help. I can work. But I can't do what you want—I'd be in hell forever, burning, and the baby would be in purgatory."

Tony remembered the first night when they had gone to her apartment after dinner—it had been their third date. Before, she had only allowed him to kiss her at the doorstep, in the porchlight, even, the bugs pinging around his ears. In the darkness of the movie theatre, she would sometimes let him set his hand on her leg and move it up slightly, slightly, until just a few inches away from her hip-swell, but that was all.

"Oh no, mister," she would say, shaking her head and swatting away his hand. That night, she'd gotten drunk from two glasses of wine—she wasn't a drinker, she said, her pretty face flushed—and had asked him back to her room. Her housemate was gone for the weekend.

"You can come up," she said, her eyes heavy, almost closed. She smiled. He saw the dark red lipstick on her teeth and had to remind himself to look back to the road, away from the dazed look in her face, the red all over her mouth.

He hadn't noticed much about her house that might've revealed more about what kind of girl she was, about how many men before him she'd let in for a nightcap. It was the usual sad bachelorette's pad, with its smell of disinfectant, and attempts at hopeful decorations like cherry-sprigged curtains and autumnal-hued fake flowers in a green, fluted vase.

Beyond the general drabness of the place, all Tony had noted was the crucifix above her bed, the sad, dying Jesus on the cross jiggling almost comically on its long, thin nail when the bed banged against the wall. He'd worried that it might fall and hit him on the head.

"Jesus Christ," he said, pulling away from her grip. Her fingernails left two long red stripes on his forearm. "You aren't going to get all holy on me now, are you? I think the time for worrying about sin is well over with."

Charlotte grabbed his arm again. She dug her nails in tighter. "I've already sinned enough," she said. "I should take my medicine. I'm going to have this baby. You can't change my mind."

She was angry with him. It was almost too much, Tony thought, that she should be angry with him—what had he done? She's the one who got herself in trouble. He looked into her eyes, which were smudged and swollen. Her lips, wiped of lipstick, were smaller and thinner than he thought—meagre, puritan lips. Her face seemed stunted, pinched. All of the softness was gone.

The hard look of her lips, how her shoulders squared against him, caused bile to rise in his throat. He didn't want to marry her—she was just a child, unable to do the simplest things. She'd tried to make him a poached egg one morning and succeeded only in burning the bottom of the pan. If he married now, he would have to support two more people. Charlotte wouldn't be able to work, not if he married her—only poor married women worked, and he wouldn't have people in this town saying he was poor.

But it would be no better if he didn't marry her. His mind flashed forward nine months, then two years. Even if he weren't with her, he would still have to send her a monthly cheque. How much would she need? He had no idea. More than he wanted to give—children had to be fed, clothed, given toys and books. He would have to visit the child, who would be a scandal. That hadn't changed, not here, where respectable people got married when they had accidents. And if he never visited the child, he would feel guilty—he would know that it was alive, somewhere, with his nose or hair, his talent for numbers. She had the power to ruin his life.

He could feel blood rising, heating his skin. The air was suddenly suffocating, hot and thick, as though he were breathing little particles of dirt and lint.

Tony inhaled, gasping, and broke free from her grip. He took her shoulders and shook her until her head snapped backward and forward. Her mouth flew open and she tried to speak. She succeeded only in biting her tongue so hard that he could see blood in the crack between her two front teeth.

He let her go and slapped her across the cheek. She sank to her knees, holding her ears between her hands, as if to keep her head on straight. Hitting her felt so good he wanted to do it again. It made her quiet, so satisfyingly crumbled.

"If you make another sound, this whole place is going to know what's going on down here," he said.

Charlotte stood, weeping, her hands over her fevered cheeks.

Maybe she feels it, too, he thought. *Maybe this room is making her head pound, making her sick, crazy.* He looked at his arm, his sleeve rolled up to his elbow—she had scratched him and drawn three thin streaks of blood.

"Now, baby, listen to reason," Tony said. He looked away from his own blood.

I have to calm myself, he thought. *I have to calm down.*

"I just want to help you," he said. "I know you aren't ready to be a mother. And what would your family think of you showing up pregnant at Christmas? Would they let you come home after you did that to them?"

Charlotte lowered her hands and looked at him, her small mouth hard, false lashes sticky and clumped together.

"I'm not getting rid of it," she said slowly. There was a short hitch in her throat when she said *it*. "I'm not getting rid of the baby for you."

"Goddamn it, listen to me," Tony started, but she surprised him by slapping him square in the chin, jerking his head sharply to the right. The violent movement of his neck caused a jolt of pain from his shoulder to chin, blinding him for a few vibrant seconds. A fine sheen of sweat broke out across his forehead.

That bitch, he thought. *Oh, that bitch.*

He turned to get the door, finally, his hand on his throat where the stretched muscles still throbbed.

She shouted, "I won't do it, and you can't make—"

"Shut up," he said evenly, trying not to raise his voice. "Somebody will hear."

"What do I care?" she screamed.

She's gone crazy, he thought. *I have to make her stop.*

Tony stood by the door, his hand on the knob. "Just shut up for a minute, Char—"

"I won't shut anything." She turned to get her purse, which was sitting atop bolts of pink periwinkle fabric. She kept talking, repeating herself—"I'm keeping it, I'm keeping it, you can't make me"—speaking loud enough for anyone at the door to hear her.

"I won't do anything you say anymore, Tony," she said.

He felt a shift inside his head, as though something was kicking at the insides of his skull, threatening to split the skin. *There's something wrong with me*, he thought, the buzzing in his head almost louder than Charlotte. He was angry. The anger hardly felt like part of him. It was foreign, but he recognized it, too, that old bloom of red at the edges of his vision.

"You aren't a good man," he heard her say, distantly, as though she was outside one of the small, slatted basement windows, shouting down at him through the glass instead of there in the room. She turned to retrieve her jacket and her voice got smaller.

"You said you would protect me. You said you loved me. You don't love anybody, you—"

Charlotte stopped mid-sentence, her mouth open. She reached to touch the back of her head, where a new pain bloomed. She felt warmth spread, drip down the back of her neck. She looked at her hands, which were covered in blood. She felt dizzy and another dull but brain-wracking pain hit her. This time, she heard, vaguely, the crack of bones.

Charlotte had time to think of how she should have gotten her secretary's degree from the women's college and worked in Albany for a bank boss or a lawyer, just like her momma had said suggested. She could have done something besides ruin her health and reputation in this factory, on a man who didn't brush his teeth, who smelled like suffocating, cheap cologne, and who didn't care one bit about her. *Oh look what he's done, that's my blood, that's my blood.* And then she remembered the baby, whom she was going to name Gabriel or Annabelle, two names for angels, and how she was going to raise him or her in the country, like she had been—away from the streets and the ugly buildings, with a garden in the backyard and a tire swing that collected water when it rained. She remembered swinging—how it had been the closest thing to flying, how it sometimes made her sick and dizzy, but she did it anyway, higher and higher, and how once the rope snapped at the height of her swing and she'd been thrown clear across the lawn and bumped her head on the ground, scraped her hands on a rock. Her mother had rushed out and cradled her and said, *Charlotte, Charlotte, are you okay? Can you hear me? Can you see me?*

Charlotte saw the red pool grow, the fluid filling the space around her cheek, spilling out beyond her nose. *At least it's warm*, she thought. *At least I can just go to sleep.*

Tony stood above her body, holding a blood-streaked brick in his hand. He dropped the brick, which splattered a few drops on his shoes and split in two.

"She wouldn't shut up," he said aloud. "She wouldn't stop talking." He wondered if she could still hear. "I didn't mean it," he told her body. "You know I didn't mean to do it."

She made no signs of hearing him—only a few slight jerks, her pumps scuffing against the hard floor.

He breathed deeply, sharply, and held his chest—he thought he was having a heart attack. The sounds in his head continued, though they were quieter, and the heat faded from his forehead, his cheeks. He could feel the cold in his fingers again.

He couldn't believe what he had done, though his arm ached from the force with which he'd thrown his hand out and smashed the brick into her skull. He looked down at the floor. *Look at what this man has done*, he thought.

Tony felt strange, outside of his body, but his mind was working again, that foreign anger dissipated. If somebody found her as she was, bleeding to death or dead already, his fingerprints everywhere, he'd be in trouble. And he couldn't get out the basement window—it was too narrow for him to get through.

He'd have to run up the stairs, go through his office, and leave out the back door. Tony looked at his watch—it was fifteen minutes before twelve. The girls didn't take lunch until twelve, and they were punctual. This was one of the virtues extolled by the previous foreman, a fat, hairless little man who'd beamed at the girls with a sexless, paternal pleasure when he spoke about them.

Tony looked down at Charlotte, her eyes wide, her mouth and nose streaming. He felt his eyes filling against his will; he had not cried since he was a child. He couldn't smell the kerosene anymore, but a headache crept around the base of his skull, one that pounded along with his heartbeat and shook his whole head.

He went to her purse and dug through the mess of lipstick tubes, tissues, pens, and lottery tickets, and found a little silver lighter. The kerosene bottle was still open. He felt the wicked twinge in his neck again, where Charlotte had twisted it with her slap.

Tony took the open bottle of kerosene and poured it on Charlotte's body. The thin, cold fluid soaked into her clothes, splashed on her face and washed away the blood. He poured some on the bolts of cloth, too, and on the floor around her.

Tony thought of explanations as he poured the kerosene. *The girls smoked down here illegally*, he imagined himself saying to the police chief, a tall, black-haired man that looked nothing like the small-town police chiefs in movies. He seemed strong and smart, and not susceptible to bullshit; Tony would have to make what he said as free of bullshit as possible. Filled with real sadness, real regret. He didn't think he'd have trouble with that.

He imagined himself tearing up, wiping his eyes, forehead in his hands. *They must have left the kerosene lid open*, he'd say. *It must have gotten kicked over, or maybe some ash fell in—it was a terrible tragedy, terrible.*

Tony mouthed the words as he rolled up his sleeves to avoid spilling anything on himself.

His back was to the door when he heard somebody call his name.

"Tony," a voice said. "Tony, I wanted to talk to you before lunch." He turned. It was Joan, the pretty, young blonde who worked on a sewing machine down with all the older ladies— tall, sweet figure, but a little bit of a snob. She opened her mouth.

Joan had decided to catch Tony early, before lunch, when he usually went across the street to Kelly's Deli. She had gone to his office and knocked on the door, but there was no answer. She then went out back, where he often went to smoke; she found nothing but a pile of cigarette butts and the river, as always, surging up and over the wheel.

The sky was grey, covered in a thick blanket of clouds. Joan crossed her arms and hugged her body close.

Maybe I should go somewhere warm, she thought. *Like California.*

She went back inside and looked around the factory—no Tony. There was only one place he could be. The basement.

As Joan started down the steps, she thought she heard somebody talking. Maybe he was in a meeting. Strange to have a meeting in the basement, which was always cold and smelled like mould.

Joan touched the door, knocking lightly. She pushed it open. Tony's back was to her. He was not wearing his jacket, and the sleeves of his dingy white shirt were rolled up to his elbows. Even from the back, he was shabby—sweat stains spreading from his armpits and down his back, the tail of his shirt un-tucked and hanging from his pants.

"Tony," she said, stepping into the basement, turning to shut the door behind her. If she had stopped to think, if she hadn't been so consumed with her task, she would have noticed the smell in the room, the static in the air.

"Tony, I have something to tell you." She looked up. He had turned, and she saw the kerosene can in his hands. The room smelled, overwhelmingly, dizzyingly, of kerosene. She held her hand to her nose. On the floor, by Tony's feet, was a woman's body, her back to the door, blood on the floor around her.

Run, Joan thought. *You have to run.* But she had already shut the door behind her.

She didn't understand what was happening until Tony took her by the elbow, jerking it out of the socket. The pain was sudden, so blinding that she could not think to right herself as he threw her toward Charlotte's body. She fell on her knees, her head resting against Charlotte's waist.

Then she felt a sharp pain at the back of her skull. Tony was more efficient this time—she felt the crack, the dulling of her senses, but not before thinking, *no, no. I am going to leave. I was going to quit today.*

I don't get to leave here, she realized as the pain lessened. Her body was covering her mind with a protective veil of shock. But still, she knew. She knew and it was too late to do anything about it. *I don't get to leave.*

Tony was out of kerosene, but he figured that the pool she'd fallen into would be enough. *Oh yes,* his mind hummed, *it will surely be enough.* He opened the basement door a crack, just enough to see into the stairway—nobody. He took Charlotte's silver lighter and touched it to the pool of blood-tinged kerosene by her hair. The kerosene caught fire, flames dancing across the fluid's surface. Her whole head was soon ablaze. Then he thought he heard Joan moan quietly.

She's still alive, he thought, but he couldn't to do anything about that, as much as he might want to give her mercy. His mind raced to ease him, to push him forward, to get him to do what needed to be done to remain alive and free. He was glad for his body then, how it could break his indecision, push him past doubt. He flicked the lighter shut and put it in his pocket. He took his keys and left the room, shutting the door behind him, and went quickly, but did not run, up the stairway. Running meant guilt. He skirted the edges of the factory. Most of the girls didn't even glance up as he passed. He went into his office, locking the door behind him, and left out of the back door, which led out to where he usually smoked a cigarette before going over to Kelly's for a sandwich. He needed the cigarette but skipped it, heading straight over to the deli instead. His cigarettes were in his office, in the desk drawer. He could see himself putting the cigarettes in the drawer—he had done so just that morning, before everything had happened, when all he'd been looking forward to was lunch and seeing Charlotte and possibly a quick nap between 2:00 and 2:30, when he could lock his door and claim he was working.

He remembered the Tony of that morning with great nostalgia. *That was the real Tony*, he thought, the sound of his own name jarring in his head, twisting and expanding with noise all around, like loud music coming through a broken speaker. He closed his eyes and shook his head. He would not listen to the noise. He would move and speak as he always did. He would be calm. He would survive.

Tony crossed the empty street to Kelly's Deli and went straight to the bathroom in the back. He scrubbed the kerosene scent from his hands, wiped the blood speckles from his shoes and shirt. He covered the blood spots on his white shirt with his jacket. Then he splashed his face with cold water and looked in the mirror. *I look fine*, he thought. *A little tired. A man with responsibilities—somebody with a lot on his mind.*

I should look different after what I've done, he thought. He looked into his brown eyes, his familiar, lined face. He imagined the girls might be evident in his eyes—everybody would know what he had done as soon as they looked at him. Isn't that how it was supposed to be—the blood would call out from his hands? That was something from the Bible, wasn't it? But he couldn't see anything different at all—he looked exactly the same on the outside as before, even though his head was screaming, even though he didn't feel that his hands were connected to his body. They burned from the sting of kerosene and the scrubbing he'd given them.

Tony wiped his face with a towel. He would go out and order a sandwich, probably a Philly cheesesteak with extra onions, and he would eat the sandwich while leafing through the *Farmington Reformer*, as he always did. When somebody from the factory rushed in to the diner, one of the girls, soot on her cheek and dress, shouting that there was a fire, he would shout at the deli owner, a fat man in overalls, to call the fire department right away. He would express the most sincere surprise. He would show his leadership by going to the girls and offering comfort. He would give them paid leave for two days and send gift baskets to their homes. He would be the kind of person he had been when he had sat down to work that morning.

Smoke began to pour from the basement almost immediately. Because the interior of the factory was constructed with slabs and beams of wood, the fire zipped up the stairwell, travelled up the wooden columns that supported the ceiling, and roared through the interior.

Fire first reached the girls who sewed on the buttons. In their small, windowless room, they did not realize what was happening until it was almost too late. Smoke poured through their open door, and when they went to find the source of the smoke, they saw fire already spiralling up through the stairway, spreading its fingers across the wall, across piles of finished dresses, running toward the main entrance of the factory floor. The women ran for the door screaming *fire!* Those who had lined up at the other end of the factory, ready to punch their time clocks for lunch, paused to watch the button girls shouting and running, the smoke pursuing behind them.

By this time, the fire had roared through the button room. It had found the piles of bolts by the foreman's office and enveloped them, the flames licking the ceiling, dancing across the rafters. The women ran, some with their time cards still in their hands. But the fire came so quickly there wasn't time to decide what was important enough to take.

Tony sat at a small, dark table well inside the deli, a table he had always avoided because it was near the bathroom, and he hated having to see people go in and out of the bathroom, hearing the door slam, hearing the toilets flush. He sat there as a punishment.

Soon enough, somebody would be coming for him. He ate his sandwich methodically, the edges first, then the middle, bursting with meat, almost too big to put in his mouth. It was oozing with mayonnaise, like the liverwurst sandwiches his mother made him as a child, like the olive sandwiches she made when they had run out of money and couldn't afford the meat she got from Gouger's market—cheap cuts of beef, chicken thighs, and liverwurst in bright red plastic. He watched sauce from his sandwich dribble out and tried to remember that he was hungry, that he'd been hungry for hours, that he had not had anything that morning but black coffee and a cigarette. Remembering the morning helped. He found his hunger again and began to eat.

When Tony saw people standing, rushing to the window, shouting *Tony, Tony*, he ran to the window. He was surprised at the shock he felt at seeing smoke pouring from the opened front door and out into the street, how frightened and sickened it made him. The women from the factory were gathered in the gravel parking lot, bent over, some retching, on their hands and knees, their stockings torn and dirty against the rocks.

"Oh God," he said aloud, with real urgency. "The factory is on fire. Call the fire department. Please. Somebody call." His voice shook. He bruised his hand on the metal bar as he pushed the deli's glass doors open. He smelled the smoke coming from the factory, a sickly, rubbery smell of burning polyester. He closed his eyes against a wave of hot, ash-filled wind. He kept his eyes shut until one of the women from the factory rushed over to him, tugged his hand like a child.

"Tony," she said, "we can't find Charlotte and Joan. Everybody else is here. What should we do?"

"We can't go in there until the fire department arrives." His voice was appropriately grave, fatherly and soothing. He would have to comfort them all with some kind of speech. "We can only wait until they come. We don't want anyone else to get hurt. And who knows? Maybe the girls ran off in a panic. I bet they're fine; everyone else made it."

She dropped his hand and they watched the fire together, the orange fists punching through the windows in long, rolling licks. Smoke poured out, the stench rolling off like dampness from a bog. The sound of sirens, which had started faintly, came now from downtown.

"Maybe, if Charlotte and Joan are still in there, the firemen will find them," Tony said. He almost meant it.

Those who survived the fire all had the same *symptoms*—that was the word their doctors used, though they rarely ventured to say exactly what they were symptoms of. *But what do I have?* The women would ask, and the doctors would shrug or sigh or sometimes make an attempt to answer, though the answers weren't much more satisfying than the word *symptoms*.

It started with headaches for most, which was normal according to all of the doctors they consulted—all that smoke, the black air they'd gulped in panic when rushing away from the burning factory, not to mention the stress, the shock to the nerves. But the headaches lingered for weeks, then months, and some even had blinding, migraine-like headaches for years afterward.

Some reported *visitations*, the strange, vague word the women came up with to explain what was happening. Some of them saw Charlotte, blood coming from her mouth and nose, holding out her open purse, which was black and empty inside. Charlotte looked weary, blood dripping from her nose and mouth and even her eyes, sticky and clumped in her carefully curled eyelashes.

And some saw Joan. While Charlotte stood, imploring, bleeding, communicating nothing, her ghost displaying her empty purse, Joan was angry. This was the one description that each woman gave of dead Joan, though the living Joan had been anything but. She'd been too cool for anger. As a ghost, she stormed in and out of their dreams, her mouth bloodied and dribbling down the front of her dress, her hair on fire. She came to the edges of their beds and shook them from sleep. She tried to speak, the women reported, but when she opened her mouth, nothing came out.

III

I

SEPTEMBER, CURRENT DAY

Claire waited several weeks to schedule a meeting with Miriam Hastings. She imagined, for a short time, that she wouldn't do it at all—why bother? What good could come from it? And why did she always rush to do what her mother told her anyway?

But the dreams continued, made her sleep as tense and stressful as being awake, made her hands shake, made her hear voices and forget if she'd turned off the oven or if she'd locked her doors and windows.

Her usual Sam dreams all took place on the night of his death, all the events happening again, slowly, in excruciating detail. The scene would begin in front of the factory as he ran for the busted basement window. She would protest, claw at his clothes, tell him, *No, let's just go home.* She would hang from him. But he laughed at her. He didn't look down. She hung from his belt hooks and he dragged her across the yard, her heels digging furrows in the soft, pine needle-packed ground. He didn't seem to notice her. He didn't seem to feel her weight around his waist. He went straight for the basement window, and she let go only as he turned to shove himself through the hole—no

matter how much she didn't want him to die, she didn't want to
go down there with him, she didn't want to fall down that hole.
So she let go, and each time she wished that she hadn't.

Then, just as she thought he would not speak to her, that she
was invisible to him in this dream world, he would look right in
her eyes and say, *Don't worry, Claire. I'll unlock the door.*

But these new dreams were different.

They kept going. She shouted down to him after he fell,
and a muffled echo came back, a blast of lukewarm air like the
air inside of a mouth, and the faint smell of burning. *Sam,* she
called, *Sam, I'm going to get you help. I'm going to get you out.*

In dream logic, Claire imagined that she could get him
out—she knew what was going to happen, that he was bleeding to death, and that in real life, the one she had already lived,
he would not make it. But her dream self believed he would
not die. Instead of going home, she would go next door and
ask them to call an ambulance. The ambulance would come in
time.

Claire. His voice drifted up, small but clear. *Claire, you can
get me out.*

I know I can! she shouted down the hole, on her hands and
knees. *I'm going to go next door.*

No, he said. His voice slushed and gurgled like water swirling down a drain. It was happening again, just like last time. *No,
I'm going to unlock the front door for you. I'm going to unlock the
door.*

As she was about to lean down to tell him that she had to
hurry, that she knew what was going to happen and she could
stop it, she felt heat unfurl from the window like a campfire
igniting under her hands, and the window's empty square lit up
orange. She pushed back to avoid the flames that jumped from
the windows. She moved backward, scuttling like a crab on her
hands and feet.

The first night, she woke kicking, her heart beating fast. The vague feeling that she could *still* do something was left over, fog from the dream that had not yet burned away. The feeling remained throughout the day. It made her feel as though she was missing something, forgetting something important, like an iron left on, the fabric beneath it burning. At work, she left her keys in the ignition and did not notice until she went out to her car at lunch to find a pack of cigarettes, to see if she still had some in the glove box from a few years ago when she had taken up a minor smoking habit. There were no cigarettes, of course, and she wondered why she wanted them. She saw her car keys hanging from the ignition and wondered what was happening to her mind.

Claire liked to visit a local café some mornings for coffee and a piece of pie. The café was right next to the library, and it had a greasy, homey, lack of self-consciousness about it that made her think of cafés in movies, places where people in town gathered and smiled and knew each other by name. Claire knew the people in the café by sight, but not by name. They smiled and nodded at her, but they didn't speak to her, not usually, unless it was somebody from the library, a regular who spent their lunch break reading magazines or browsing the stacks.

"Do you know what you'd like?"

A girl not more than seventeen or eighteen was at Claire's elbow. Her apron was splattered with orange grease and her badly dyed hair was held up in the back with a pencil.

"Just a coffee and some peach pie."

As the girl turned and walked away, Claire saw Marcus walk through the door, the little bell on a string jingling against the glass behind him. He smiled at her before she could get up and leave, could sneak out the back door into the little alley between the café and the dry cleaners. She forced herself to smile at him. When he smiled in return, his face lifted and lit up and she felt sorry all over again for what she had done to him. She waved him over.

We'll be friends, he had said the night she asked him to leave. It wasn't a question, but a plea. He had held her hands tight between his. He'd even cried, in a silent, involuntary way that made her feel even worse than audible sobs would have. She had, right then and there, wanted to take what she had said back and invite him to unpack his clothes from his shiny, never-used luggage. It was a handsome leather set he had gotten from his mother as a college graduation present, in anticipation of a year of post-college travel. The travel never happened, and that night he had stuffed his clothes—soiled, clean, folded, balled up, some still on the hangers—in the sweet-smelling bags, pulling out balled-up filler paper as he went.

Of course we'll be friends, she'd said. *You are one of my best friends. You always will be.*

She hadn't spoken to him in five months. At first, he left messages on her phone. Then, the messages ended, and she'd assumed that he was angry with her, that he didn't want to try anymore, and she was grateful. Obviously, she'd told a lie that he should have understood as such—they couldn't be friends.

"Claire, it's so good to see you!"

Marcus opened his arms and she stood, accepting his embrace. He smelled good, like toothpaste and shampoo. Marcus had dark, almost black hair and eyes the colour of slate—he was the only grey-eyed person she had ever met. Though he was at least six inches taller than her, he stooped, which made him seem shorter and somehow friendlier than most tall men. She learned after commenting on his stoop that he corrected his height to match whomever he happened to be with. He didn't like to make people uncomfortable, he had told her, though he knew that slouching was bad posture and that he'd probably pay for it someday.

This was what she had loved about him: his give. It was also why she made him leave.

"It's good to see you, too," Claire said, as the waitress returned and set down her coffee and pie.

"Would you like something, sir?" The waitress looked irritably at Marcus and poised her pen above the pad in exaggerated readiness. She didn't like surprises, Claire thought. She knew the feeling.

Marcus smiled. He didn't see that he had annoyed the waitress—he didn't notice things like that. He assumed that most people were pleasant, inviting, and did not harbour irrational anger. Claire had often admired his ability to not notice other people's moods while also being completely irritated by it. How wonderful it would be, she often thought, to only have your own emotions to worry about.

"I'll take a coffee and a number three," he said.

The waitress nodded and left them alone. Marcus turned his smile back to Claire. He gave it away freely, that smile. He was, Claire thought, the kindest person she had ever known. He probably had no ulterior motive for coming to sit with her that morning.

"How've you been, Marcus? How's work?"

Marcus worked at the municipal building. He was the grant coordinator and spent his days writing extremely logical, orderly, and almost indecipherable documents to beg various government organizations to give Farmington money. Claire used to go to his office on her lunch break, as the municipal building was only a few blocks from the library. His office was in the basement, in a small, windowless room that had once belonged to the town's short-lived peak oil committee.

"It's the same as always," Marcus said. "Nobody wants to give us money. The office is completely bare now because I finally got the all-clear to throw away all the peak oil stuff."

Claire smiled. "You should hang up a motivational poster or something. A kitten hanging from a tree limb, you know, *hang in there, baby,* or one of those aerial photos of Farmington they sell at the fair."

Marcus thanked the waitress, who set a cup of coffee by his elbow and a plate of eggs and bacon in the middle of the table.

Claire wondered if the girl thought they were on some strange, morning date. They probably seemed, from an outsider, like people who did not know each other very well—smiling awkwardly, making weak jokes, searching for words as they stared at their food. Claire speared a chunk of her peach pie and chewed it. The crust was soggy and gummy, and the peaches tasted like cheap jelly. Now that Marcus had destroyed her calm, she wondered why she'd ever found the place charming.

"But how are you, Claire?"

She cleared her throat and sipped her coffee. When she had asked Marcus to leave, she told him that she felt her life was stuck and stunted, and that she was good for nobody until she found out why and how to dig herself out. And then, she'd explained that she missed feeling strongly for him. She didn't say *I don't love you anymore,* but this is what she had meant. She said that he deserved better, and that he was the best person she had ever known. She had meant that part.

He had looked at her with the same concern he seemed to have now, only then it had been touched with confusion and anger. He hadn't known dissatisfaction as intimately as most people, and had been surprised by her decision to end the relationship.

Are you depressed? he'd asked her, grasping for words to attach to what she was feeling. Claire didn't know how to answer. She liked her job. She felt a satisfaction in her everyday life, the humming from thing to thing, in walking down the sidewalked streets, but still she felt that she should let Marcus go. He was comfortable in the way her big, king-sized bed was comfortable. She loved that bed because she had gotten it cheap and it was an easy thing to sink into. And that was her problem with Marcus, too.

No, she had told him, *I'm not depressed. I'm just in a rut. I just need to be alone for a while.*

"Oh, the same as always," she said. "I teach the elderly how to surf the Internet. I shelve books. I pet the cat. I'm the same Claire I've always been."

Marcus chewed and looked at her thoughtfully. "I'm glad to hear you're the same," he said. "That Claire was always good enough for me."

She looked down at her pie.

"I was thinking lately of what you said, about feeling stuck," he said. Claire wondered why Marcus had been thinking about her life or things she'd said. She had scarcely thought about him at all.

"Have you ever thought of leaving Farmington? Of living somewhere new?"

Claire looked up from her pie, the broken mess on her plate that she couldn't bear to finish. She looked out the window, at the sun flooding the streets, the people as they rolled down their sleeves, feeling the edge of autumn on their exposed skin. She watched a little girl, maybe six, with a metallic purse, skip by her mother's legs, which switched back and forth, back and forth.

Farmington was her town. She loved it here. She loved it because it was as familiar as her own body. And sometimes, like her own body, she wanted to leave it behind for good.

"I don't know," she said. "I can't. This is where I live."

"But it doesn't make you happy to be here, does it?"

"Why would you say that?"

Claire tried to imagine herself in another place. She had visited other places, of course. New York City as a college student, and Boston as a child and teenager—her parents took her and Sam there each summer to show them pieces of history, plaques and museums, like the ones in Farmington, only bearing the names of people she had read about in history books. They were nice to visit, but being away from Farmington made her restless. She wished for her own bed, for the view from her window, the streets she recognized. She loved Farmington. Every place she walked now was a place she'd walked as a child. She had seen the CVS turn into the organic food store, then into the tuxedo rental store.

But there were other reasons, too. It wasn't her parents, whom she loved the way that most people loved their parents, but no more. It was Sam, of course. He was still here. She had lost him here. The idea of leaving meant leaving Sam behind.

Marcus picked up a piece of bacon with his fingers. "I don't think this town is good for you," he said. "Too many ghosts. Too much past." He chewed and swallowed, not taking his eyes from her. She had the urge to put her hands over her ears like a child, to block out his voice, but she didn't. She stared back at him. At least she had her anger.

"I don't want to leave my ghosts," she said. "I don't think my ghosts are a problem. I love my ghosts."

Marcus shook his head. "When you forget for just a minute, I can see it, you know? Your face clears, and you're really looking at things again. But that happens so rarely." Marcus reached his hand across the table and took hers. His hand was dry and cool, and she felt no passion in his grip. He felt sorry for her—that was all. She felt a faint prickle of sadness, somewhere in her stomach, at this change. Once, he had been angry at her, had left shouting messages on her voicemail, and now all he felt for her was pity for the person he believed she had become—almost middle-aged, a cat-lady without even the ambition to have more than one cat. Even her eccentricities weren't impressive.

She closed her eyes and hoped that she would not cry. She didn't like public displays of emotion—they seemed cheap and unreal, and she didn't want people in the café to know that the librarian had been weeping in the local greasy spoon at eight thirty in the morning.

"I like it here," she said. "That's all. It makes me happy. I don't need your pity." He tightened his grip. His face registered disbelief. *Christ, how does he see me?*

Maybe I should leave, she thought, *just to see what it's like. Just to see how I would be in another place.* She slid her hand from under Marcus's. She imagined herself in a place with no winters, in a strapless sundress, her hair lighter and longer; her body collapsed in the loose weave of a deckchair, like in a commercial for a cruise ship. She looked over his head and away from his concerned face, suddenly pleased with this image of herself—this other self, doing nothing at all in a sandy, sunny landscape that shimmered with the possibility of beauty in some form she couldn't even imagine. She hadn't entertained such an idea of herself before. She was not the kind of person who travelled. Nor was she the kind of person who made plans on a whim. But she could be. Maybe it was time. She said none of this to Marcus.

"I'm sorry," she said. "I just don't see the point of this conversation right now. I don't need advice. I'd just like to have breakfast with you, okay?"

Marcus nodded. They finished their breakfasts and exchanged more cordial questions and responses. She imagined that he had a new lover—that would explain it. A new lover would allow him to speak to her the way he had, with brotherly concern instead of passion. It would allow him to feel sorry for her without being angry.

They hugged goodbye. The embrace was tight but cold.

She hoped she wouldn't see him again. All his generous pity. His brotherly concern.

* * *

She continued to dream every night that she could save Sam. Sometimes the dream was preceded by others, dreams that were clearly misfirings in her mind, as most dreams were—where she was flying, or falling or had shown up to a college classroom for a test without any preparation. But then, she was always back at the factory again, Sam running ahead of her, heedless to her cries. And every morning, she woke with the thought that it was possible to save him, if only she could stay in the dream longer.

The dreams were a constant buzz in the back of her mind, an inner alarm going off, telling her that something had to be done. Sometimes she even came home from work during her lunch break and wandered the apartment, lifting envelopes and pieces of paper from her coffee table, picking through the trash, looking for something that her mind insisted she had forgotten. She checked the stove, the bathroom for an iron plugged into the wall. She had daydreams of her apartment burning while she was filing away books, the cat darting under chairs and tables, smoke filling the rooms. Her hands shook. She bought another pack of cigarettes and kept them in her glove box to take the edge off.

After a week of dreams, a week of restlessness, Claire woke one morning and saw the front page of the *Farmington Banner*, which proclaimed that the Beans construction and remodelling of the old factory was about to begin. The local construction company, Daily Brothers, had been awarded the contract. The article emphasized that Beans, according to district manager Justin Hemmings, would be trying its best to work with local businesses and community members. He said that the company wanted *to practise business in a way that gives back to the community that it depends upon.* Justin Hemmings spoke in perfect sound bites, Claire thought. She wondered if he had visited the factory—she thought that a visit would have dispelled him of any notion that a business could be run in that building, that people would willingly go in and out of those doors. A photograph of the factory, empty, the chains on its front door visible, took up a full fourth of the newspaper page—pointlessly, as everybody in town already knew exactly which factory it was.

That night, she dreamed again of Sam and the fire. This time, she had stood back and watched from about five feet away as he lowered himself into the hole, smiled up at her, and disappeared. The slate shingles seemed to hiss and steam and turn slightly orange with heat. She stayed back, though her body told her to go to him. She refused to give the dream what it wanted. She clenched her fists at her side. She didn't move as the flames shot from the window, as the wind blew and rattled the hanging chains against the door.

I will stop this, she thought. But not on these terms.

She woke weeping, her face feverish in the otherwise cool room.

That morning, she drank her coffee in the kitchen, over the sink, the windows open, blowing damp air through the house.

I can't make it go away, she thought. *I can't stop it on my own.* She imagined the factory opened, redecorated, people walking the floors, laughing and talking and sipping expensive coffee, and closed her eyes. The image was unbearable. She would talk to Miriam Hastings.

II

Even before the fire, parents had told their children not to play out past where the sidewalk ended, where Factory Street became Route 9 and spread out, the road banked in tangled weeds, plastic wrappers, and faded soda cans and beer bottles twisted in the mess of green. But it wasn't just because the factory was at the end of town, at the place where it became farmland and wilderness. The factory also pushed up against the edge of the river—behind the factory, the ground dropped in a steep, grassy hill that ended at a short, muddy, rock-dotted shore where the river began. It wasn't safe. It wasn't a deep river, but the bed was littered with boulders, and if you fell from the top of the hill, you would most likely bust your head on a rock, or at least break a bone. Every few years a teenager, drunk or just stupid, would try to jump into what looked like a deep part of the river and break their body on the rocks.

Soon after the factory was first built, children began to tell stories about it. When the dirt in the entrance was still criss-crossed with wheelbarrow imprints and footsteps, the children whispered that the missing girl, Sally Shaw, had been buried there—you could see a spot where the earth was piled in a little Sally-sized lump, where somebody had stomped their boots down to smooth the dirt. Like all children, they were sometimes pitiless, fascinated by what terrified adults—murder, ghosts, blood, a child buried just feet away from where they played.

Long after Sally, during the war, children whispered that at night, if you went past the factory, you might see the man who lived in the basement—he crawled in at night to sleep. It wasn't that he'd done anything wrong, anything criminal; it was that he was crazy, and though he might seem normal for long stretches of time—he might even accept help, an invitation to dinner, or a warm winter blanket—he was always really on the verge of something violent and unexpected. Though the children didn't know much about madness, they had seen insanity in movies. The mad shuffled and bit, they screamed, they pulled their hair and hurt themselves: they could not be trusted.

The parents, their minds less adept at telling stories, made vague noises about why the children should avoid the place. *The air is damp there,* was a common reason. *It's damp and cold, near that river, all of those bugs, all of those rocks, the nails and boards, the sharp drop out behind that place, you could break your arm, you could break your skull . . .* But the parents heard the stories that the children told, and they matched not what they knew, but what they imagined: yes, it seemed like the kind of place where a child might be buried under the loose dirt and furrows, where somebody might lunge at you from the darkness with a broken beer bottle.

So the stories continued, though there was nothing specific to pin them on, no central image to bind them—not until the fire. Then there were ghosts to match the place. Women who crawled from the basement windows to grasp your ankles with their dusty, charred hands; women who crawled from the river (where they slept to cool their flaming skin) and squelched after you, their feet bloated with river water, their burned skin forever sloughing off.

III

The *Farmington Banner* arrived at Sunnydale at five every morning, and those who could still read the paper unassisted—who could shuffle to the activity room in their slippers, take their cup of pills from the woman in bright scrubs, her hair redolent with freesia, and sit in the activity room to read or watch the television or play chess, checkers, or if the weather was sweet and warm, sit out on the screened-in patio—read the *Banner* each morning from front to back, lingering on the obituaries, the Dear Abby columns, the articles about children and their 4-H animals, photographs of young women and men holding hands, smiling into the camera, their engagements official.

Richard, almost ninety, who still took walks every morning after his juice, pills, and paper, opened the latest issue and stopped at the front page. He touched the page and ink came away on his fingers. The factory.

Others shuffled in: Cyndi dragging her walker across the rough carpet, Arthur, who was rolled in by Miss Chester, a young, busty woman who gossiped and sometimes spoke loudly on her cell phone in the nurse's station, and a few other stragglers. Richard looked up and waited until they passed and had settled into their seats, the televisions turned to their favourite station, which played only game shows, all day. He resisted the lure of game shows, but he found himself, sometimes, peering over his spy novel or newspaper, wondering if those nice people on screen would win a trip to Bali if they could only arrange the prices of various grocery store products in the right order. To avoid the noise, he went out to the porch, though the air was cold for August, and unfolded the paper again.

So they were rebuilding the factory. A coffee shop. Revitalization. It all sounded very cheerful.

Richard remembered the day of the fire. *A fire at the textile factory*, his mother said, her ear to the telephone's mouthpiece. The voice on the other side was probably one of her friends, one of those women who knew everything there was to know in Farmington—who seemed to have chosen their houses based on the visibility of adjacent points of crisis: the fire department, the local dive bar, the police station, the high school.

Joan, he thought.

He had spoken to Joan the week before. She'd been at the grocery store, buying milk. They had exchanged pleasantries. He remembered she had been wearing a yellow skirt and a white button-up shirt; she was dressed like a girl on a date, though she was only buying orange juice. It seemed strange, then, that he couldn't walk up to her and take her hand, as he had so many times before. She did not seem angry with him, and he could not manage anger at her. She had simply grown tired of him, her in her bright dresses, her secrets. There had been no theatrics, no arguments. Before Joan, he had never had cause to doubt himself; he had always been enough. But she had simply let him go without any protest. It had been his first serious wounding, though he had never admitted it.

He drove to Factory Street, where he could see a billow of black smoke rising over the pines that lined the river. Fire trucks blocked the street, so he parked at the steel mill and walked to the factory, behind the trucks, cutting through a backyard to avoid the firemen who were waving away bystanders. A group of women huddled near the trucks, though a fireman told them to *stand back, stand away*. A few police officers skirted the perimeter, holding the women back.

He couldn't see Joan. Maybe she had left, seeing no purpose in standing around in the poisonous smoke. Maybe she had been sick at home that day, flipping through her movie magazines in the attic room he had visited so often, back when she wanted to see him. He imagined her in the room, her window open, her cheeks blazing from the constant heat.

He lingered for a few minutes more, but there was no sight of her. He left the way he had come and drove home. His mother asked him if he had seen Joan and he said no, but he hadn't seen much at all.

Nothing to worry about, he had told her, patting her on the back. Joan could always take care of herself. He was sure that she would be fine.

He attended the funeral in the awkward position of being the former boyfriend who some people, mostly her older, more distant relatives, still assumed to be a current boyfriend. Richard nodded and comforted those who came to him. People couldn't place him—he must be feeling something, but they didn't know quite what. So they kept their distance, and he kept his. Her closed casket was black as a banker's shoe, and the bundle of white lilies on the lid drooped in the too-warm room. Later, after the funeral and weeks of mourning, upon seeing Joan's mother in the street, taking her small, ladylike steps, he did not go up to her and say hello—he went the other way, often dodging through alleys, around the backs of buildings to avoid her. Sometimes he saw Patricia in the grocery store, wrestling with one of her thin, perpetually whiny children. He didn't have to go out of his way to avoid her—she seemed to be in a fog of annoyance, too absorbed by her children and the problem of feeding them, clothing them, and getting them from the grocery store to the car to worry about him or anyone else.

And so he drifted out of their lives. After five years, nobody asked him about Joan. After ten, it seemed strange to him that it had happened at all. He remembered Joan, but mostly in colourful pieces—her dresses, her lips, her fingernails. He remembered that she laughed more often than anyone he had ever known, but often at inappropriate times—during serious films, or when he was describing something he didn't intend to be funny. And he remembered that he hadn't been enough for her.

Later, he married a woman with Joan's affable personality, her figure, but none of her nebulous ambition. Leslie was satisfied with what he could give her—a large house in North Farmington, a housekeeper every Wednesday and Friday.

When he travelled for insurance assessments, for conferences, he found women that reminded him of Joan in hotel and airport bars, sipping from their glasses, their faces open and wise. They had no interest in holding on to him. The first time he took one up to his room, a woman with high, wide cheekbones and lips pink as crayoned petals, he was terrified—what if she somehow discovered his home phone number? What if she became pregnant? What if she wouldn't leave in the morning? What if she cried and said she loved him? He had to muster up the courage to touch her when she slipped out of her dress.

He needn't have worried. She left efficiently and completely, thanking him for the drinks, smiling with her bare lips, revealing a row of crooked teeth. And that's how they all were. Like Joan, they weren't really interested in him—he was only research, preparation for something that Richard wasn't a part of.

He sat out on the sun porch for a half-hour, until the cold seeped through his sweater.

He sometimes imagined Joan's ghost. He didn't really believe in ghosts, but Joan had seemed a ghost even before she'd died—a creature he couldn't quite catch or remember really touching.

They should let her rest, he thought, rising to go back inside, maybe watch some of those quiz programs or play checkers with Buck. He doubted, though, that she was resting. She had never cared for resting.

Miss Chester, or Jackie, as her friends and family called her, read the article over her rushed doughnut and orange juice. She ate from behind a pane of glass, where she could look out into the activity room without having to listen to the constant noise of the television, of wheels or teeth working, of the *shuffle shuffle shuffle* of slippers.

The factory. Her first personal memory of death was tied to that factory. Even before her grandparents, before distant great-aunts or pets, Sam had died. He had been in her class, a popular boy who had always been kind, if dismissive. She had been overweight, not unpopular, but not popular either—merely a fixture, one of the mass of people who went together from class to class, not as friends but with a peculiar loyalty from spending eight hours a day for most of the year in the same rooms.

He had died down there in the basement. He had fallen, maybe, broken bones, bled to death. It had seemed impossible to her at first. Sam dead? He was too healthy to be dead. She could remember him running laps around the track as she sat in the bleachers, reading *Seventeen* and feeling invisible.

When the knowledge set in, when she attended the funeral and saw the heaps of flowers, his parents in black, bent and pale, she became afraid for herself. Sam, a familiar part of the room, a voice she neither delighted in nor feared, was gone. But what was worse was how—it could have happened to anyone.

I could fall down the front steps and die, she had realized. *A car could hit me as I'm crossing the street, humming to myself, thinking of dinner. It isn't up to me at all.*

She'd never quite gotten over that knowledge.

IV

Justin booked himself into the Farmington Hotel for a week. He had come to check on the construction of the building, that's what he told the foreman, but he had also come to test himself: would he crumble this time? He had also scheduled a meeting with Miriam Hastings, the Assistant to the Town Manager. He had found her photograph on the town of Farmington's website: tall, slim, a blonde bob. She had gone to the state college for a degree in Human Resources and had been a resident of Farmington for her entire life. Justin had written her small biography on an index card and highlighted things he could discuss—her human resources experience, her small town life, what it was like to be married to a doctor, her children. Asking people about their lives endeared them to you, he'd found. He had been a shy, awkward child, unsure how to *be natural* with people. Learning tricks like this had helped.

Justin drove down streets named after presidents and trees (*Lincoln, Garfield, Poplar, Cedar*) and saw where the simply nice neighbourhoods became the good neighbourhoods, became the wealthy neighbourhoods—houses that sat on large plots of elaborately landscaped yards, with gates and trees and cobblestone driveways or three-car garages. He had his eye on a little white house on Maple Street, just blocks away from the factory, a starter house with an expansive backyard fenced in by a secure, but friendly, red picket fence. *A place for children to play*, he'd thought, though he had no children and knew that Karen didn't want any right now.

I don't think I'm ready, she'd told him.

This had ended the conversation, but Justin persisted in imagining his future child—a shapeless, sexless, uncertain thing, mostly a flicker of movement in the corner of his eye, the idea of a room filled with toys, superhero-themed sheets, and glow-in-the-dark moons and stars affixed to the ceiling.

Karen didn't want to move to Farmington.

Fine, she had said. *You go. Spend a week there. See how much you like living in the middle of nowhere. I'm staying here.*

He had not argued with her. He knew her life was in Albany—her yoga classes, the women she had lunch with, the various people she spent her days with that he had never met, phantom people named Joey or Connie or Claudia whom he sometimes heard stories about. It made him jealous that these people, who didn't seem real, could make her happier than he could.

Justin didn't understand himself: she was right, of course. Their lives were there. She liked Albany and saw no reason to leave. He was being unfair, forcing her because he had made an enormous choice for them. But what else could he do? It felt like fate. He moved forward. He tried not to think about Karen as he struggled to sleep in this unfamiliar room. He remembered the basement instead, what it had done to him.

Being in the basement had reminded him of when he was a child and his parents, having saved up enough money for a rare treat, had taken him and his brothers and sisters to one of

those enormous waterparks filled with big plastic slides, children in bright bathing suits with inflated balloons on their arms,
and over-priced snacks and soda. He'd wanted so badly to ride
the biggest slide, and his parents finally let him, but on his way
down, he'd gotten twisted in the plastic tube and was spit out, his
limbs akimbo, and smacked hard into the surface of the pool,
the chlorinated water filling his mouth and lungs. He thought
he might die, but he had somehow made it to the surface and
saw his father there, laughing, and had pretended nothing was
wrong. Of course, the basement was really nothing like that: at
no point had he really been in danger. But that feeling remained,
of being close to danger and having nobody to tell.

Justin woke in his room, a honeymoon suite with white lace
accents, scented bubble-bath bottles in a shell-shaped bowl
in the bathroom, and a guestbook by the bed, signed by former couples who had stayed there. He read the honeymoon-
ers' names as he put on his socks and shoes, lacing them tight.
Heidi and Joseph. Caroline and Glenn. Alfred and Connie. He
couldn't put a face to any of them, couldn't make up a story. He
could only imagine them in this bed, under the covers on their
wedding nights, pulling up the tight sheets from between the
mattress and box spring to move more freely, throwing off the
comforter, bulky as a winter sweater.

Justin opened his files, checking for each necessary document: the contract, sales receipts, insurance paperwork. He
placed each document in the correct file and laid each file
neatly in his briefcase. As he entered the rental car, which
smelled like hospital pine disinfectant, he imagined his files,
the coloured tabs zipped tight in the mesh compartment of
his briefcase, the row of capped pens all in working order. He
felt himself calming as he made the sharp turn off of Main
toward Factory Street.

At the factory, a man about Justin's age stood by a black truck. He leaned against the shiny black paint, arms crossed, and stared out at the forest across the road. Justin recognized him from high school—not him exactly, but his type, the person who could look out over a classroom full of new people and feel absolutely no anxiety. Even the man's stance was at ease, his face untroubled as Justin drove up and parked. Justin imagined he was the kind of man who knew his place in the world exactly.

The man's name was Chris. He was the foreman. He shook Justin's hand.

Justin glancing over Chris's shoulder to the factory's door. He felt his palms and the back of his neck going cold and sticky.

"Let's go inside to take a look," Justin said.

Chris nodded. "We'll have to talk about the basement," he said.

"What about the basement?"

Chris cleared his throat. "Awful stench down there—maybe a mouse crawled in and died, maybe a bird, something like that. The guys can hardly stand to be down there for the stink. We'll have to do something about it."

Justin nodded. "I noticed that too, the last time I was here." He put his hands in his pockets. He had the urge to spit, to make Chris feel that they were alike—he was just a regular guy, not irrationally afraid of a basement or the smell of a dying animal.

"Let's go check it out," Justin said.

Chris nodded and walked toward the factory, its doors thrown open. Inside, the formerly murky main room was alight. Debris from broken machinery and office supplies had been gathered and placed in a heap by the entrance.

The factory floor was still a jumble, filled with cords trailing from saws and drills. The workers ate their lunches on a rickety folding table.

Chris and Justin went straight back to the small, sturdy basement door.

"Your vision for the floor area is clear," Chris said. "A cashier at the front, four sections, a wide-open space toward the back, the wide windows, all of that, but the basement is tricky. The space is there, and I imagine you and your company don't want to waste it, but it makes for a lousy storage area. Dank, narrow, all that." Chris motioned toward the door. "Let's go down."

Just as Justin remembered, the air was thick with dust, but it lacked that particular electric, sickening, *alive* quality that had sent him out of the factory the last time.

It smelled stale, rotten, and wet, yes, but not alive. He breathed in deeply, almost savouring the hints of mould, burnt hair, excrement. He could handle this.

Chris grimaced, holding his hand over his nose. "See what I mean?"

The basement was still full of machines draped in tarps, tied down with ropes thick as a thumb, the knots so old and tight that Justin imagined they would have to cut through them to see what was underneath. But the shapes were clearly those of machines and nothing else. He breathed easier. He put his hands in his pockets and rocked on his heels. He wasn't afraid.

"Well, it doesn't smell good, that's for sure. But that can be fixed, can't it? Can't you find the source?"

Chris looked around. "It could be an animal, dead somewhere under these tarps. Or maybe just rot in the tarps themselves—mould can smell like something dead. I can't be sure."

Justin nodded. He was in charge. The man was looking to him for guidance.

"Empty the whole place out," Justin said. "Get rid of it all."

Chris nodded, squinting at the sudden light blazing through the basement's tiny windows as a cloud rolled away from the sun.

Justin watched the dust-thick air as the sun illuminated each little particle.

I am not afraid, Justin thought. *There is nothing to be afraid of here. It's just a room.*

V

Miriam Hastings did not take bullshit. This was what people said about her, and she approved of this assessment. It was a vision of herself that she'd cultivated. *I don't take any bullshit*, she said once during a meeting, and now people repeated it and believed it. It was that simple. Now that the town officials knew her better, knew that she wasn't afraid to call the police chief a son of a bitch or tell someone to shut up during a town meeting, people even said it to her face, as a compliment.

That was how she had risen so far in a town run by men. She didn't let people speak down to her, speak over her, speak as though she wasn't in the room. She wasn't aggressive, she wasn't an asshole, but she made her presence clear. She thought of it as projecting herself. When she sat down to a meeting, she imagined that her body was three times its actual size. She imagined her presence was solid and certain, absolutely inviolable, a fact of nature. Then, she could speak her mind.

Miriam was the first woman to hold the position of Assistant Town Manager, and though she was officially a step below the Town Manager, it was common knowledge that Miriam was whom you saw if you wanted to get something done. Dick

Stevens, the Town Manager, was a good face for the town, a good man to have at museum openings and public ceremonies. The Stevens family filled the Sunnyside Cemetery with their elaborate, fenced-in clusters of gravestones. There was even a monument for one of the family's particularly rich patriarchs— an angel perched atop a stone slab, her clothes draped across her body, wings folded tight at her back.

Miriam had gone to the graveyard for lunch during her teens. She remembered sitting on that tall stone fence, thinking of how silly it was to waste such a pretty statue in a graveyard. Now she worked for the grandson of that illustrious dead man, and she'd recently passed a law to keep people out of the cemetery unless they were there to mourn—no more joggers, lovers, or kids having lunch.

Miriam remembered Dick Stevens from high school. He had been one of those blond boys with perfect teeth, boys who did everything with ease. He didn't remember her and had been surprised to learn that she'd gone to school at Farmington High, just two years behind him.

"I thought I knew everyone!" he'd told her. She'd only nodded. He had known everyone worth knowing. Back then, Miriam had not yet become no-bullshit Miriam. She'd been sad Miriam. Small Miriam. Miriam-in-waiting.

The seeds of Miriam's adult self were planted during her eighteenth year, when her father died silently in bed. Miriam's mother had woken to find him cold beside her, his mouth and eyes open, his face surprised. *That was the worst thing*, she had told the children, *how surprised he had seemed*. Miriam wished she'd never been told that detail, but her mother had lost the difference between things you keep to yourself and things you tell your children.

After her father's death, Miriam's mother no longer attended Mass, not even on holidays. Following the funeral, after his things had been packed away, dispersed, or given to charity, the family moved to a small apartment in downtown Farmington, away from their little white house; the rent was too much for Patricia after her husband was gone, and she didn't like being far from town anymore. Living in town meant that she could shuffle from her front door to the corner store to buy packs of gum, Wild Rose wine, and cigarettes, which she smoked, pack after pack, while watching game shows or staring out the kitchen window into the street.

Although Miriam could have left, she stayed home for two more years, until her younger brother was eighteen. She didn't trust her mother to watch him carefully enough, to keep him from doing something stupid and killing himself, like so many boys did. It seemed that every month, a young man ran himself off the road and into the lake, or got so drunk he fell asleep on the railroad tracks. After she'd seen her brother through his teenage years, she applied to Farmington College, an all-girls school hidden back in the green hills just north of downtown, well away from the factories and convenience stores. She had seen the college girls downtown as a child, remembered wishing that she could be their age, walking around alone on the streets, free to do whatever she pleased. They had armfuls of books. They laughed in the windows of coffee shops and restaurants. They were lovely and alive and Miriam wanted to be more like them than her mother, who shuffled through life in stockings with a widening ladder of runs.

Miriam had done very well in school—better than her siblings, most of whom were a few points away from failing. School tired them and left them irritable; it was almost a given that they would drop out before graduation, to begin working. Miriam, on the other hand, loved school. If possible, she would have stayed in school through Christmas vacation, maybe curled up under one of the heavy wooden tables in the library, wrapped in a blanket, books about Africa and the Salem Witch Trials and French poetry scattered around her.

She received a hefty scholarship from Farmington College, one of the first schools in the area to give scholarships to underprivileged young women.

"But how will you pay?" her mother had asked.

In her mother's world, everything cost something, even if they said it was free. When Miriam explained about scholarships, about how she was willing to work to support herself, Patricia looked down at her lap and shook her head.

"You're too much like Joan," she said, "and you know what happened to her. That's what her plans got her."

Miriam missed Joan. She remembered her well, how she talked and moved, the swish of her skirts.

After Joan died, her parents had found a bundle of money under Joan's mattress—over two hundred dollars. They also found her notebooks, her scribblings of stories and plans.

Miriam remembered that she had cried violently at Joan's funeral—ridiculously, her mother had said, enough that everyone stared at them. It wasn't just that Joan was gone, but that everything Joan had planned was gone, too.

Joan had died when Miriam was eight, just the age when she was beginning to understand the permanence of death. Sometimes she would lie in bed at night, curled under the thin blankets, and imagine what would happen if her mother died, if her father flew off the road while speeding (she never imagined him dying in bed, asleep, as he would many years later), or if she died suddenly from something tragic and wasting, like leukemia or tuberculosis. She imagined the casseroles and bread that the neighbours would bring, how the house would be darker than usual, dirtier because nobody would remember to clean, the dishes piling up and clothes spilling from the hampers. She imagined a time of things being unmoored and irregular, the usual rituals of home ruined and made obsolete with the absence of just one person. She imagined her own death, which she could only experience as a soft, dreamy slipping away, a fall into something like the fuzz after television stations ended.

Joan's death had been nothing like that soft retreat: it had been an explosion. Suddenly, a person who had no business being dead was gone, along with everything she had ever felt or wanted, all of her personal memories and the constant narration in her head, all of it. The thought had terrified Miriam, but it had also prepared her. The world will constantly take things from you. So you have to push to get what you need while you are still alive and able.

When Miriam first learned about Beans, she had been distracted by a small crisis—a police officer had tased some protester in the parking lot of the local power plant, which caused an outcry in the community. She'd only seen a memo posted on a sticky-note on her computer monitor about permits for a new establishment in the old slate factory.

Later, when she sat in bed with the day's paper, she saw the front page, the photograph—it was the New England Textiles factory, looking much as it had fifty years before, and a short article about the company Beans, a high-end coffeehouse that had bought the property and was beginning to remodel the interior. The article had quotes from somebody named Justin Hemmings, whose words were amusingly optimistic and empty, full of wonderful opportunities and benefits for the community, all of that bullshit that marketing and business people had to say and perhaps even believed.

Miriam put the paper down on her lap, brushing the edge against her husband's chin. He moaned in his sleep and turned away.

She told herself that she had no reason to be upset. The factory wasn't only Joan's factory—she couldn't claim its tragedies for herself. There was no logical reason why she should feel alarmed. But she was alarmed.

After the fire, long after the factory had been fully restored, becoming one of the largest employers in the area, a series of accidents occurred that caused the factory to be shut down for good. A crate of batteries had exploded in the basement, injuring a few employees. Several had come down with mysterious illnesses, later determined as resulting from the unsafe handling of heavy metals. It was also the place where a teenager had died, what, fifteen years ago now? Miriam had been the program director at the Boys and Girls Club then. The boy had been well known, well loved, though she had never met him.

And now, this company was coming to give Farmington more customer service jobs, more minimum wage workers. Miriam shut the paper. If Justin Hemmings really wanted to help Farmington, he'd bring back the textiles factory, the steel mill, all of the jobs that had once made the town prosperous. But that was ridiculous, too: those jobs didn't even exist anymore.

The day of her meeting with Justin, Miriam wore her pearls, her powder pink suit with stockings, and the shoes that pinched her feet.

"You dressing up for a lunchtime rendezvous?"

Harry pinched her elbow. After thirty years of marriage, they felt safe making jokes about adultery, as they were both too busy and too tired to even consider an indiscretion. She simply smiled in response. Her hands shook that morning, and she feared if she spoke she might say something unexpected. She might cry. She was doing something good for the town, something she had been hired to do: she was welcoming in a new business. But she didn't have to like it.

Miriam checked her makeup in her compact and sniffed her wrists to make sure that the perfume was not too heavy or too faint.

"You look good, Mom."

Her daughter, Jennifer, was in town for the week. Miriam had hardly been home—it was the end of the fiscal year and she spent most afternoons bent over ledgers and spreadsheets and indecipherable budgets while Jennifer watched late-night television, still in her pyjamas, often with a carton of ice cream in her lap.

"Thank you, sweetheart."

Miriam almost wished that Jennifer had not come to stay. She had awakened that morning feeling afraid and guilty in an incoherent, lingering way that she'd only previously experienced after a night of bad dreams or too much drinking. That night, she had dreamed about her aunt Joan, about the factory, about the fire, and the boy's death. The dream stuck with her.

She sipped her orange juice. It touched a raw spot on her lower lip and stung.

Jennifer paged aimlessly through the previous day's *Wall Street Journal*. "You know," she said, "you look ten years younger than your actual age."

"That's good to hear," Miriam said. She wondered if it meant anything to look younger than sixty. After forty-five, did it matter anymore?

"You're quiet this morning," Jennifer said.

"I'm sorry, honey," Miriam said. "I just have a very big meeting today. Somebody who might be very important to the town. Somebody I can't disappoint."

Jennifer nodded as she broke a single Pop-Tart into pieces and ate each piece slowly, worshipfully. She now liked to eat the kinds of foods that she was never allowed to eat as a child.

"You'll knock him dead," she said. "You look just like a president's wife."

She laughed. "I'd rather look like the president."

That morning, the Fire Chief, Dwayne, gave Miriam his weekly roundup of activities. Beans was working on bringing the old factory up to fire code.

"It's a big job," Dwayne said. "The whole thing. The wiring in there is ancient. But Justin is determined. Have you met him yet?"

Miriam shook her head "We're meeting later today," she said. "Have you heard anything about him?"

He nodded. "He wants to make himself a *genuine part of the town*, that's what he said to Chris." Dwayne rolled his eyes. "He wants to be on good terms with *the movers and shakers*. He said that too." He smiled, and Miriam wasn't sure if he was mocking Justin Hemmings or if he approved of such naked ambition.

"I'm not sure I like that location," she said, observing Dwayne's response: she didn't want to sound fearful, irrational. "You think that anyone will come out to that old place? You remember the stories they told about it in school?"

He nodded. "I heard that a while back one of those paranormal shows even wanted to come in and do some kind of nonsense with the factory. Bring in some psychic in a shawl, you know, have her use her tarot cards or something. But the owner wouldn't give permission—he didn't think the town needed that kind of tourism."

Miriam sniffed. "The town needs any kind of tourism it can get," she said. She kicked off her shoes, which pinched her feet and gave her a blister on her left big toe. "It's not like we have a lot of people who want to come look at our plaques celebrating places where generals stopped to feed their horses," she said.

Dwayne snorted. "Guess that's true." He looked at Miriam. "But you know how it is—we like to keep to ourselves. We don't like people getting into our business. About the factory, though," Dwayne shrugged. "I guess it can't hurt to try," he said, getting up to leave Miriam to prepare for her meeting. "I don't think you'll ever find me there, drinking a six dollar latte. I remember the stories too well. I don't need nightmares."

Justin was much younger than Miriam had expected. He had short, blond hair so thin and pale that his reddish scalp showed through. His eyes were a bright, freakish blue. His face was unlined.

He can't be much over thirty, Miriam thought.

Justin rose and pressed his hand into hers.

"Wonderful to meet you," he said. "I have heard so much."

His hands were clammy with perspiration. He smiled widely, the skin around his lips stretched thin.

"Please take a seat," Miriam said. "We aren't very formal here."

Most people liked to hear this—Miriam had seen people sink down in the seats, the tension in their shoulders dissolving after she absolved them of the need to watch themselves so carefully. Just the expectation of formality made some people hunch and pinch and shiver.

But Justin only nodded; his head jerked back and forth mechanically like the top of a Pez dispenser. He sat severely upright, his shoulders thrown back like a Miss America contestant doing her stiff walk down to the microphone. He wanted badly to impress her, Miriam could see.

"I thought I'd schedule a meeting with you simply to get to know you," he said. "I'd like to make it clear how much I love this town, how much I want to be part of it. Beans is my way of giving something back."

Miriam couldn't help but smile. Privately, she didn't understand patriotism, all that flag waving and an unflinching belief in one's superiority due to birthplace, but she understood loving a town, a particular piece of land. She loved Farmington, too.

"I'm glad to hear that," she said. "I've lived here my entire life. I can't think of anywhere else I'd rather be."

"I wish I could say that about my own home town," Justin said. "I left there as fast as I could. You're very lucky."

Miriam nodded, but didn't ask him about his hometown. She assumed Justin was here to get some kind of information from her, to complain about the permitting process, to in some way get his project moving forward more quickly. He would probably appreciate brevity. "How is the construction going so far?" Miriam asked.

"Fantastic," Justin said. "It's coming together perfectly. Some electricity issues, and the basement is a problem, but other than that, fine."

Miriam nodded, waiting.

Justin beamed. "We're trying a completely new model here in Farmington. The factory really is a perfect location—close to downtown, on a major scenic highway to the closest city. It's exactly the kind of place we were looking for."

Miriam had sat through many pointless meetings before with small business owners. Usually, they wanted to get to know her in order to grease the wheels of local government, to make their faces and businesses familiar so that maybe, at some point, they could call in a favour. Miriam didn't give favours. But she realized that this wasn't why Justin had made the meeting. He wanted something else from her. Perhaps her approval.

She didn't know how to give it, so she simply kept nodding and listening.

"I was worried," Justin said, "when I first found the location. The owners seemed . . . hesitant. I've heard things about the factory. That it has a history." His eyes dropped and he became fidgety again, his hands twisting in his lap.

"It does," Miriam said. "I'm sure you've heard about the fire. The later deaths."

Justin nodded.

"That's one thing that worries me about the location," she said. "If I'm being honest. I wonder if people might be hesitant to come to a place of business where so many people have died in very tragic ways."

Miriam heard her words as if from a great distance. She hadn't intended on talking about the factory's history at all, but it came out anyway.

"I think you'll find that people will be happy to come, if we can offer something they want." Justin assured her. He leaned in closer, his hands on her desk. His air was intimate, knowing, as though he were telling a secret between the two of them.

"To tell you the truth," he said, "that factory called out to me the first time I saw it. I knew it was meant to be our next location. It's too beautiful to waste, all boarded up, a haunt for ghosts and a place for kids to come smoke pot and drink cheap liquor from paper bags. It should be used, shouldn't it?"

Miriam didn't know how to respond. *It called out to me.* It called out to her, too, but in a different way. Nobody seemed to have a normal relationship to the factory. You'd never say that an abandoned Wal-Mart called out to you, that a combination Taco Bell/Kentucky Fried Chicken was clearly *meant to be*. But here she was, listening to a man she'd just met speak in vaguely supernatural terms about a building.

"It sounds like you've thought this through," she said, finally, unsure if this was what he wanted to hear.

"I'd like your support," he said. "I think of Farmington as my town, already, and I want to do what is best for it."

Miriam nodded. There was little else she could do. Why wouldn't she support him? Because her aunt had died a half a century ago in that building? Because the idea of stepping into it for a coffee sounded about as appealing as swimming in the river behind it mid-winter? Often, in her time as the Assistant Town Manager, she'd had to agree to things she did not truly want to do. But they had never before been so personal, and so strange, as agreeing to support a coffeeshop in the place where her aunt had burned to death. But what other choice did she have?

"I'll see you at the opening," she said.

Joan had died fifty years ago. She was gone and nothing could be done about it.

He smiled. "Thank you for the opportunity to be part of your town," he said.

After Justin left, Miriam shut her door.

"It'll get better," she said aloud. She imagined her aunt Joan in the room, sitting where Justin had been with her legs crossed, her hair sculpted into something elaborate and icy.

"I'm doing this because I have to," Miriam said. Her aunt wasn't there. Her aunt was in the Catholic cemetery, her grave long untended.

Perhaps Justin was right. Perhaps it was time to make the factory right again.

VI

Claire woke to the smell of mint. Not a subtle smell, like something drifting in from an open window, but a smell like a sprig of fresh mint. She remembered that sensation, that burning.

She sat up in bed, laughing.

"Sam, get out of here!" she shouted into the empty room.

She closed her mouth and covered it with her hand. She was in her apartment, not her teenage bedroom. Sam wasn't breathing on her face, trying to wake her up. He hadn't done that in over fifteen years because he was dead.

She sat up in bed, the cold air leaking in from her open window. During the day it was as hot as August, and she had to strip down to a t-shirt. At night she pulled on her sweaters and warmed her feet with the small space heater in her room. September didn't know where it belonged.

Claire threw off her covers and went to the kitchen. She was completely awake now at five-thirty in the morning, hours before she needed to be. She busied herself with making coffee, scooping heaping tablespoons into the fluted white cup, pouring the water, scouring yesterday's coffee cup and mugs and saucers. Rarely plates—she hardly used plates since Marcus left.

She ate yogurt out of plastic cups and sandwiches off of folded paper towels.

Claire went to the kitchen window and threw it open. The dust from the mini blinds blew into the cold, clean light, making tiny twists and curlicues in the air.

She took a cup of coffee and a handful of chocolate chip cookies to the living room. The window there looked out at the rows of houses across the street, all two-storeyed and well-manicured. Decorative gates surrounded some homes, while others had Tibetan prayer flags in the windows or papier-mâché masks hanging from the trees. College students lived in this area—mostly older students who shared houses, made small gardens, kept compost heaps. A deep, even sidewalk ran along both sides of the road. Farmington was a walking town, and usually Claire could see college students walking, joggers, women pushing enormous strollers. There was nobody out now, though, not this early. Claire sipped her coffee, which was thick, black, and made her back teeth hurt.

Today, she was meeting with Miriam Hastings. It had taken her two weeks to make the appointment, and then another two to find a time that both she and Miriam could meet. She had a half hour of Miriam's time—a precious amount, she knew, but far too little to explain exactly what the matter was. She had told Miriam that she had some *concern* about the factory and the new company, but she had not specified her concerns. She imagined that Miriam thought she was just one of the many people in town who objected to the corporate ownership of a historical town building. Claire had seen the picketers in front of the town offices earlier in the week.

Claire was happy to let Miriam believe that this was her concern. She felt stupid going to Miriam, like a frightened child going to her mother after a nightmare. She didn't have a real reason, nothing she could explain clearly or succinctly, just a sickness in the pit of her stomach when she imagined teenagers sipping coffee feet away from where Sam had died. And her dreams had compelled her, of course, which she couldn't tell Miriam about.

At six, Claire rose from her couch and dressed. Her neighbours, an elderly couple who still held hands when they went on walks, led their three small dogs down the wide sidewalk on gold leashes. They cooed and spoke to the dogs like children. Claire could hear them from inside her apartment, even when she went to her bedroom to dress, or into the ill-lit bathroom to apply her makeup. She practised her speech in the mirror. She would sound merely concerned. She would sound sane.

Miriam was afraid. She didn't know why, but she didn't want to meet this woman who worked at the library. However, when she was appointed Assistant Town Manager she had agreed to meet with any and all concerned members of the town. She had said this on television during a local broadcast of a Select Board meeting. She had made herself the friendly, available face of the town, the person that any normal citizen could petition and expect a fair hearing.

So she brushed the crumbs from her doughnut off her jacket and prepared herself to meet this Claire.

Why are you so nervous? Miriam looked at her face in the pocket mirror, smudged her eye shadow out of the crease of her eyelid and wiped the lipstick from the edges of her mouth, where the colour bled into the surrounding wrinkles.

Her secretary knocked on the door.

"Your next appointment is here."

Miriam nodded. "Show her in."

Claire recognized Miriam from the newspaper and from the town picnics that the library employees attended every July, along with the parking staff, the planning department, and the historical society. She had shaken hands with Miriam twice, was twice graced with her easy smile, but she was sure that Miriam would not remember her. She had priorities far higher than remembering some librarian. Claire was used to being the kind of person that nobody made it a habit to know.

Miriam wore a neat, grey suit, but she did not look severe. She seemed warm, smiling generously, her eyes friendly.

Claire felt the heaviness of her long skirt, the awkward way the seams of her blouse lay across her skin. She wondered what she would look like in twenty years. She imagined she'd share more in common with the women who wore elastic-band pants and boxy button-up shirts while shuffling around downtown in their garden shoes than she would with Miriam Hastings.

"Wonderful to meet you," Miriam said. She stuck out her hand. "You work at the library, right?"

Claire nodded. "For almost ten years now."

Miriam dropped Claire's hand and gestured toward the doorway. "I recognize your name from the timesheets," she said as she clicked ahead of Claire in her heels.

Miriam's office was warmer than Claire expected. The walls were painted yellow and covered in photographs of handsome, active children alongside plaques and certificates with Miriam's name in calligraphic script, honouring her for her work raising money for the Boys and Girls Club and her contribution to the Humane Society Walk-Run, and her award from the Chamber of Commerce for most civic-minded local politician of the year. Not a particularly hard award to win, Claire imagined, but it was something.

"What would you like to chat about?" Miriam folded her hands on her desk, which was littered with paper and a half-eaten doughnut, and leaned forward. "I hear you have some objections to the new business opening in the old textiles factory."

"Well," Claire licked her lips. "Understand, I'm not opposed to it for the reasons you might think."

Miriam nodded, encouraging.

Claire's well-planned speech disappeared from her mind completely. "I just think," she said, "that the town should have had more notice. The people of the town, I mean. Through the newspaper, through a special town meeting. We should have known. We should get to decide. It's not like any other building. You know that."

Miriam nodded and smiled.

"Many people have this confusion about the plan," she said. "The town isn't taking over the building—it is actually a privately owned factory—"

"No, I know," Claire interrupted. She shifted in her seat. "Excuse me. I didn't mean to interrupt, but I know it is privately owned."

Miriam nodded. She gave the impression of having endless, bountiful patience. It pained Claire to try such patience.

"I know it doesn't belong to the town," Claire said, "but I think because of what happened, you know, because of all of the accidents, that we should all get some say in what happens to the place. I mean, all of us that have been affected by it. Those of us who've suffered because our loved ones died in there."

Miriam's mouth opened slightly. Her carefully drawn eyebrows shot up. *She thinks I'm talking about her*, Claire thought.

Claire shook her head. "I mean, my brother, Samuel," she said. "You might not have known this, but my brother was the teenager who died in the factory fifteen years ago."

She looked down at her knees again. She'd said his name. She hated to say his name—particularly to people that had not known him.

Miriam flashed fear—she pulled her lips away from the edges of her teeth in a slight snarl and her eyes went big. She tried to correct this quickly, before Claire noticed. She had to be careful: this was the kind of situation that could quickly elevate into a *scene*. She also had the desire to reach out and hold Claire's hand, to tell her that she understood, that she had the same fears, the same desire to leave the factory chained up and abandoned. But she put on her Assistant Town Manager face. She said what she had to say.

"I understand your concern," she said. "And I'm so sorry for your loss. I, too, lost a family member in the factory. It was years and years ago, and nothing as painful as what you have experienced, but I can understand why you might be upset about the town allowing the factory to be used as a place of business again. But those accidents happened in factory settings—places where fires, industrial accidents, all sorts of risks are possible any day. We just happen to have more than our fair share of tragedy."

Claire nodded. "I understand that."

"And, really, the town has nothing to do with it," Miriam went on. "It is a private building. Unless you want to try to declare it a historical site or a memorial, which is unlikely to happen, there is very little we can do. I'm sorry."

Claire couldn't think of anything else to say. She had known all of this before. She didn't know exactly what she wanted from Miriam Hastings.

"I hope that you, and other concerned members of the town, will try to see this as something to help make those memories, that history that has been so painful to so many of us, finally the *past*."

Claire looked away, trying to control her face. Miriam could immediately see that she had said the wrong thing.

"I don't want the memory to go away," Claire said. "Losing those memories means losing my brother."

Miriam shook her head and held up her hands.

"I assure you, that's not what I meant." She sighed. "I meant that the town as a whole would be better, happier, if the factory could be a generative, useful place again. Not just a building full of ghosts."

Claire nodded. "I know you didn't mean anything by it," she said. She cleared her throat and rose. "Thank you for your time."

Miriam stood as Claire made her way to the door. She had lost Claire, had made her feel ashamed and vulnerable. But what else could she have said? She stood, helpless, and watched Claire leave.

Claire paused in the doorway. "I dream about him now," she said. "I do want the dreams to go away. As much as I loved him, as much as I don't want to forget him, I can't have him here all of the time, always reminding me. Maybe I want the ghosts to go away, too, but putting some goddam *coffee shop* in the factory isn't going to get rid of them."

Miriam simply stood at her desk, nodding. Later, she wished she'd said something about her own doubts. But she couldn't. She was in charge. She had to keep her power.

"I'm so sorry for your loss," she repeated, her desk a barrier between her and Claire's grief.

Claire nodded and shut the door behind her.

Miriam sat down again at her desk and tried her best to let the meeting go. There was, after all, nothing she could really do: she wasn't the local therapist, she was the Assistant Town Manager. She looked at her agenda for the day. She finished her doughnut. She continued making the town run smoothly.

VII

The breakup had happened smoothly, almost easily, though not without the necessary skirmishes and proxy wars—Karen's complaints about uncapped toothpaste and Justin's grumbling about opened nail polish bottles that were really about things too difficult to articulate. They had all been rather gentle, half-hearted attempts at causing trouble, as though both knew they were playing parts, that this was a necessary pre-show before the main event. It seemed somehow wrong to merely agree to part, divide things, to shake hands and wish each other well. So they made some fuss, made a few mutual friends uncomfortable, and staged a dramatic breakup scene at a restaurant. Karen had wept into her cloth napkin. Justin had drunk three large glasses of red wine and felt a sickening mixture of elation and deep regret. *Look what I've done to her*, he thought, her candlelit hair blurring into the wallpaper behind her.

That night, they lay in bed crying, apologizing to each other for not being quite the people they should have been. The next morning, they had calmly decided that Justin would leave by the end of the week. He would sleep on the pull-out bed in the living room. She would immediately begin to look for a job in advertising, something to do with art. She spoke enthusiastically about this.

Justin had known that it was coming for weeks, maybe months. She didn't want to align her life with his, not now that he had made a choice without her. And he couldn't make her. Her being there in a little house in Farmington, angry, wishing always that she was elsewhere, would kill his happiness. He remembered that life of waiting, being miserable and trapped in a small house where he did not belong with people who understood nothing about what he wanted. That had been his childhood. He didn't want Karen to know how that felt.

Karen had been baffled by his decision to move to Farmington.

"You don't *have* to go," she said. "But you want to go, to leave everything we have here. To leave me. And I don't know why."

Justin didn't know either. When he saw Farmington in his mind he saw it from a distance, as he had when he first drove over the mountain—that little bundle of houses, the distinctively New England church steeple rising from the centre of town, the Farmington Monument like a grey sword against the blue sky, forests of dark pine trees. He had wanted, even then, to enter the town, to live in that sweet picture that he'd seen from a distance. It was like a postcard. It was the kind of place that one might call *idyllic,* though Justin knew that these paradise places only existed for visitors: that town in the postcard didn't really exist.

Still yet, he had loved it from the moment he stepped out of his car, when he walked across the gravel at the New England Textiles factory. He loved it more than he loved Karen. That, of course, had been the problem all along.

Justin pulled into the factory's parking lot, which was now almost empty. He was meeting with Chris again. There had been a minor hitch earlier in the month when they'd had to change crews. Justin wasn't quite sure why. Something about squeamishness, allergies to chemicals, it was all unclear. Chris had assured Justin that those problems had been resolved, and that the new crew had been completely satisfied with the job.

"They were local guys," Chris had said by way of explanation. "The place spooked them is all."

Since Justin had visited last, the weather had started to change. The air sounded brittle as it went through the trees, their leaves still mostly green (though darkening, getting heavier and greener before they turned). He crossed his arms over his chest. He had not worn a jacket. He thought it might be a sign of weakness to wear that puffy, unseasonable thing just because of a little cold. He had also left most of his winter clothes in Albany, with Karen, who had cheerfully assumed control of the apartment and all of the expenses.

I'll pack the sweaters for you and you can pick them up when you come back to town again, she had said, smiling as though he had given her a gift and not a chore.

She had seemed happy then, a woman lit up having suddenly solved a nagging problem.

He was setting her free. It made him sad to think of himself as a particularly heavy burden, but he guessed he was.

Chris emerged from the doorway. "Good to see you again." He shook Justin's hand. "We've made quite a bit of progress."

"Has the basement improved?"

Chris grinned and nodded. "You'll love it. Nothing spooky about it."

Justin didn't love it, but it wasn't the place he remembered. It smelled of bleach and lemon. The walls were still their muddy brick, but that was to be expected—they couldn't wash away that dirty texture or the colour of old blood. New fluorescent lights shone from their little white cups along the ceiling. The room could no longer be called damp or dark. It was almost bright. It was almost cheerful.

"I'm impressed," Justin said. He stepped back, toward the doorway. The smell of lemon, the heat, all that light, was making him sick. But he didn't want to seem ungrateful.

He touched the railing with his hand, put one foot on the last step. He breathed shallowly, wiped the fine sheen of sweat from his forehead.

"So we're on track for the late October opening?"

The foreman grinned. "Absolutely."

Justin had rented a small home near the factory. It was tucked back near the woods, away from other houses. He moved into the empty house with his books, his clothes, a few scattered plates and cups, and a television. He left everything else to Karen. He wanted to show her that he did not have hard feelings, that he cared for her and wanted what was best. It was surprisingly easy to do this. Months before, he couldn't have imagined himself leaving so quietly and without despair, just a heavy sadness, a realization that they had put so much time into each other for nothing.

Justin didn't consider himself to be a religious person, but he felt things. When he stood in front of the mailbox, he often knew exactly what letters he would find inside; when he stepped into a room, he usually knew who would like him, who wouldn't, and who he wanted to like him and would have to pursue.

He had his goal, his vocation—he would make the factory right again. And already he was succeeding: the basement had been bleached clean, the trash cleared away. It wasn't the same place he had entered just a month before.

He spoke to the men who were putting up the last-minute trimmings and blocking out the counters, the floor space, and the dining area. Soon they'd be painting—creamy walls with deep red and brown accents, indicating coziness and comfort, or so the colour consultant had promised. He had already put advertisements for positions in the paper: *bright and friendly employees wanted, a positive and energetic job environment, potential for advancement.*

Justin walked around outside the building, as he often did when he visited the factory. He crouched by the riverbank, watching the water rise and fall over the rocks below. The water was clear, cold, and clean—cleaner than any pond or pool or lake he'd swum in in his adult life. It reminded him of his childhood, as many things in Farmington did.

Justin had swum in rivers as a child, in cold, shallow streams that came down from the mountains. His mother would park by the side of the highway, in a worn-out space where fishermen and swimmers had parked for decades. She sat on a rock and read romance novels as he and his sister splashed in the water and rearranged the rocks to create shallow little pools to paddle in.

I don't know how you kids do it, she'd said, waving them away when they came close enough to splash the fake tan from her legs. *It's freezing. I'm surprised you don't catch pneumonia.*

It *was* freezing. Justin recalled that he'd work himself down gradually, inch by inch—first his feet and ankles, then his knees, his thighs, up to his belly button, and then his chest. The arms were somehow the worst.

His sister just hopped in all at once. *It's better this way*, she'd said. *You get used to it all at once.*

Justin watched the strange way the water whirled, riding the bumps and crevasses beneath it like a blanket over a body. Across the narrow river behind the factory (the length of two cars, easy to cross when it was low and placid), a thick block of evergreens edged the opposite bank. In all of the time he'd been out there he had seen only one person on the opposite side—a girl, weaving through the trees in a white dress like something from a painting or a 19th-century poem. She was not more than twelve, dressed in a gauzy nightgown that flew out behind her as she ran between the slim tree trunks, right along the edge of the bank.

The river smelled like salt, like dirt, and sometimes like blood, when the wind rose and carried its deeper smells up the bank. It curved and carved through the ground and didn't care what it swept away.

When Justin couldn't sleep at night, he went down to the river in his striped pyjamas, holding his flashlight and a sleeping bag in a bundle in his arms. He'd sit at the edge and listen. The river was different at night—you could hear things that were hidden during the day, like the small splashes of an animal entering the water or something rushing past the evergreen branches on the opposite bank, the pine needles swishing against its fur. He'd close his eyes and listen: when he couldn't see the water flowing, it sounded strange and unlike anything he had ever heard before, like the continual crumpling of soft paper or small hands clapping in a constantly changing rhythm. He could fall asleep to the sound.

I belong here, he thought. *Not just in this town, with these people, but right here, at this river, in this particular place in this particular moment.*

After her meeting with Miriam, Claire discovered that she was angry. It wasn't an emotion she indulged in often, so at first she mistook it for sadness, then for the onset of a cold (a shakiness, a scratchiness in her throat). But no, it was anger. Not so much with Miriam, who had a job to do after all—she had to do what was best for the town and couldn't very well refuse to support a new business. Claire knew this. She was not unreasonable.

Claire was angry with herself.

You never stopped being afraid, she thought. She had let the factory make her so afraid that she couldn't walk past it, could only drive past—behind all that steel and plush and glass in her car—when it was absolutely necessary. The factory was the centre of the feeling that spread to everything in Farmington. Everything reminded her of Sam, of the event that had taken him.

I can't be free of it while I'm still here, she thought. Marcus was right.

But she also couldn't leave, because Sam was still here.

When Claire spoke to her old friends, the people she had known as a child, she knew that Sam was there with them, too. They were thinking of him, how handsome he had been, intelligent, bound for somewhere wonderful. It would have fine for her to stay in Farmington and work in the library and run Internet classes for the elderly if Sam were still alive. It would have been a good balance, with Sam out there somewhere in the world, coming back at Christmas and Easter with stories of where he had been and what he had done.

But without Sam, she was a tragic figure, a person of almost a criminal lack of ambition. She should have done something big enough for the both of them.

But Sam wasn't really gone, was he? He still seemed to be here, in whatever form he had now. He could even wake her up—the mint, the pressure of his elbows on her shoulders, the slight sandpapery texture of his chin against her cheek. The year he'd died he had started to grow facial hair in that patchy, tentative way of teenage boys, their cheeks mangy and thin like old carpet.

Claire stood in her bathroom, the bright bulb carving shadows into her face, furrows and hollows where there hadn't been any before. She was naked from the waist up. She touched the thin skin around her mouth.

"Sam," she said out loud, staring into her own eyes. "Sam. Why won't you leave?"

What would they have in common anymore, anyway? He would be fifteen forever, in love with Pearl Jam, skateboarding, building model bridges, and drawing the complicated mechanisms of bicycles and engines in his notebook.

Nobody answered her. She hadn't expected that anyone would.

Claire picked fuzzy, pink lint from her sweater and pulled it over her arms. She put on her A-line black skirt, her opaque stockings, and her shoes that clicked, then twirled her hair in a bun and pinned it back. She then gathered her purse and keys and started walking to work, thinking, *why won't you let me leave?*

Before Sam had started coming back to her with such insistence, she had believed herself a person who had lived an *examined* life. She was never going to be famous or exceptional, and she had made peace with that. *But I haven't examined everything*, she thought.

Claire had not been near the factory in years. There hadn't been much reason since the factory had closed down, since that whole road had gone to seed and all of the grand old houses had been sectioned off into apartments, turned into places where people parked rusty cars in the yard, hung *Beware of Dog* signs on their fences, and strung clotheslines across weedy backyards.

At the end of the day, she shelved the last library books, tossed a ripe apple from the horror section shelf, pulled a long, handwritten letter from a copy of *Women in Love* and tucked

it in her purse to read later, pushed the books tight to the edge
of the stacks and held them fast with the book stop, and all the
while thought, *I'll visit tonight.*

It was getting darker earlier. The change always seemed to happen too quickly. Claire drove with the windows up. The sun had
already reached the very edge of the horizon, edged the clouds
orange, sent a harsh light into her eyes.

She drove slowly down Factory Street. It looked the same as
she remembered—rows of factories before the river, that grey,
busy ribbon behind the squat blocks of buildings. Then the slate
factory, a storey higher than the others around it.

She parked in the empty driveway. The doors were locked
with a heavy deadbolt, just like they had been the day that she
and Sam had come, only now the deadbolt was clean, new, and
the windows were clear. Claire walked to window closest to the
door and pressed her forehead against the glass, shading her
eyes from the glare with her hands. Inside, the sun cast beams
of light in fading stripes across the floor. It was bare, panelled in
a light oak. Claire squinted and strained to see past where the
light illuminated, to the back of the building—maybe there was
still a door to the basement. She wasn't ready to crouch down
and look through the tiny basement windows. She didn't even
like to stand near them—she imagined a hand reaching from the
window, grasping her ankle, pulling her down through the slit.

"Excuse me."

Claire started and stepped quickly away from the window.

The man standing opposite her was in his early thirties. He
wore a business suit, black shoes, a blue button-up shirt with no
tie. His hair was pale and short, his skin sensitive, pinkish, like
a baby's, as though his skin was missing a layer.

He said, "I'm sorry to have scared you—"

"No, I'm sorry. This is probably illegal or something. Trespassing on company property." Claire motioned to the Beans sign that had been stuck in a churned mound of dirt.

The man shook his head. "Oh no, it's not illegal to look." He glanced past her, at the building, backlit by the sunset. He smiled at the building as a man might smile at his own child putting together her first puzzle.

A month ago, she would have excused herself and hurried away to the safety of her apartment. Her hands shook. She stood with her back to one of the tiny basements windows. She badly wanted to escape, but she did not move. She wouldn't give in to fear. She would face this, finally.

"Do you work here?" Claire asked.

The man nodded and held out his hand. "I'm Justin Hemmings. District Manager for this new branch of Beans."

Claire took his hand. It was warm. "I've heard about you," she said. "I've seen quotes from you in the paper."

Justin nodded. "Your town has been very kind to me so far. Are you a local?" he asked.

Claire nodded. "I am as local as they come. I grew up just a few blocks away from here."

"So you've heard the stories."

Claire swallowed and clasped her hands in front of her skirt. Her arms made a heart-shape over her body.

"About this place?"

Justin nodded.

Claire watched him as he stared at the factory's black windows. It looked blank now, devoid of history.

"Those stories upset me," he said. If he'd been a boy, his voice would have cracked.

"This place is beautiful," he said. "It's hard for me to believe that other people don't see it, too. Just look at it."

She looked. They were losing light. In the dark, the factory looked as though it had been shingled in slices of heavy, low-hanging clouds.

"But it has a history," he said. "It's hard to simply see a building when you know the history."

"What do you know about it?" she asked him.

"I know that accidents happened here. I know that people died." He looked to his feet and cleared his throat. "But I want to make the kind of place that people don't associate with those things anymore, you know? As a local, don't you wish that this could just be a place of business again?"

Claire swallowed and nodded. If she didn't look at him, she could remain quiet.

I need to tell him who I am, she thought, but her mouth wouldn't cooperate.

"I was just here to see how the construction is going," she said. "Sorry to have disturbed you." She turned away from him. This was enough, she thought. Enough for one day. When the place opened, she'd come inside. She'd order a coffee and make herself sit down and read the paper. Slowly, she'd cure herself.

"Wait," he said. "Would you like to come inside? I can show you around."

You can't go in there, don't go in—a voice pleaded. She was not entirely sure if it was her own. Her stomach made a sound she hoped only she could hear. She felt the skin of her palms go sticky.

Don't be afraid.

"Sure," she said. She held her voice together by force, moving her mouth emphatically around the sounds. "That would be wonderful."

The key to the factory was on his personal keychain, among house keys and a small, silver key to a post office box in Farmington. Claire had one just like it, for the post office box where all of her magazines and junk mail went. She visited it weekly, sifting through the magazines, advertisements, and pleas for money from various organizations. It was comforting to see a similar key on his keychain. Nothing terrible could happen in the everyday world, where little keys opened post office boxes and men in khaki pants almost broke into tears over retail property.

She followed him up the concrete steps to the entrance. A light switched on automatically.

"We'll have to put guardrails in next week," he said, pointing to the steep drop at the sides of the steps. "Safety regulations." She stayed close to his back, lightly grazing the fabric of his jacket when she reached the top step and the flat expanse of the porch.

He's right here, she thought. *Nothing can happen with somebody else right here.*

Inside, she could see nothing, but smelled fresh lumber and lemons. He flipped the light switch. Rows of fluorescent lights flickered and steadied, filling the factory with the bright, greenish light.

The factory looked completely new from the inside—there were no signs of the old textile machines, the conveyor belts, or anything else that would mark it as what it had been before.

"The coffee shop is in the back, right?" Claire pointed to the very back of the room, where stools surrounded a high semicircle bar and small tables were staggered along the floor, shiny metal outlets on the floor beneath them.

He nodded. "It's going to be great—I see there isn't really a coffee shop in Farmington, not a place where people can come and sit and linger. Diners, sure, but nothing besides that college coffee shop in North Farmington. None of the locals go there and it's so far from everything but the college."

He walked slowly across the floor, pointing out the empty display shelves. "Here we'll have our collection of signature chocolates, here will be our ground coffees, here the t-shirts and handbags."

Claire nodded, trying to hang on to his words, though her skin crawled and she felt suddenly itchy. She breathed deeply, listening to the sound of the air coming in and out of her mouth. She balled up her fists and refused to scratch.

Look, she thought. *I am here and I am all right. Sam, I'm okay. I don't need you anymore.*

"So, does the factory have a basement?"

Justin turned to her. He had been explaining the eco-friendly lighting system, how a small windmill on the roof of the building would light the three fluorescent bulbs at the coffee bar.

"Why?"

Claire forced herself to shrug. "I think I heard about one, back when this was a factory. Just stories. If you believe this place is haunted, then the haunting would be in the basement, for sure."

Justin nodded. He was very quiet for a moment.

"You believe in ghosts?" he asked.

She shrugged. "I don't know. It would be fun to see though, wouldn't it?"

He looked away from her, fidgeting. "Fun," he repeated. "It doesn't sound fun to me."

"It's not important," she said. She had frightened him. "We don't have to look."

He shook his head. "Oh no, I'm just trying to remember exactly what we decided to do with it," he said. "I'm not sure if it's ready yet."

He's lying, she thought. He looked up at the ceiling after he spoke, the first time that night he hadn't met her eyes. She wondered why he would lie. Maybe he had ghosts of his own down there.

"I think it's just a storage area." He nodded. "Yes, we're just keeping boxes down there. Not good for much else. I can take you down there if you want."

All at once, as though the memory had opened up around her, Claire felt the warm air from the basement on her face, heard Sam's raspy breathing echoing far back in her ear, slipping around like water after a swim.

"I've got to get going," she said. "Maybe another time."

He shook his head. "No problem. I'll walk you out."

Outside, it had become almost night. Stars materialized in the eastern half of the sky. They hung over the river, their reflections blurred and fragmented on the water.

Justin paused by Claire's car.

"I rarely ever do this," he said. "But what the hell. Would you mind going out to dinner with me sometime?"

Claire didn't immediately answer, and she felt him growing flustered.

"You grew up here," he said. "I'd like to get to know some people from the area. I live right around here, just up the road." He pointed into the darkness, beyond the streetlight next to the factory. He lived past where the town sidewalks stopped. Where the town proper ended. It wasn't safe, or so she remembered hearing over and over as a child: *Don't go past the sidewalks.*

"Of course I would," she said. "It must be hard to come to a new place like this, to know nobody."

Really, it seemed a dream to her. How lucky it would be to live in a place where nobody knew you, where nothing reminded you of anything but itself, where every street, and building, and face was new and might take you anywhere.

He said that he would pick her up. She hoped that he would leave first so she could stay and look at the moon on the water, could summon up the bravery to crouch down at one of those small basement windows and peer inside and see nothing, but he insisted on telling her goodbye until she was forced to get into her car and drive away in the dark.

Claire thought of Justin as she undressed. She undid the buttons on her shirt, unable to remember the last time she had unbuttoned her shirt with any urgency. For that matter, she couldn't remember the last time that somebody else had unbuttoned her shirt for her.

She liked Justin, what she knew of him, which wasn't much. She liked his face, his calm, his apparent love of Farmington. Claire stood in the dark, her blouse half-undone, her white bra a flash of brightness in the opposite window. Like the last flash of Sam's teeth when he smiled before he pushed himself down into the basement.

Justin took her to the only restaurant in town with cloth napkins. This was how The Chelsea was known in town—*that place with the cloth napkins*. A good place to bring a girl, his neighbour had told him.

When he went to pick Claire up, she had made him wait in her living room for fifteen minutes.

She sat in the bathroom, calming herself. Then she paced her bedroom for a few panicked minutes, afraid that she had left something embarrassing in the living room, like a vibrator in the desk drawer or an issue of *People* magazine on the lampstand.

I'm as nervous as a teenager, she thought. She picked her clumped eyelashes apart with the hooked file attached to her nail clipper until each lash was free and she was calm enough to go down.

He held open the car door for her, then the heavy glass restaurant door. He even pulled out her seat at the table. She blushed and shrugged as he pushed the chair to meet her body. She had never had a man do this for her. She felt like a spectacle.

She noticed her high school history teacher at a nearby table, eating clams. He smiled at her; he probably wouldn't know or remember her had Sam not died the year after she'd been in his class. She could feel familiar eyes on her, people she had known since she was young, by face if not by name.

Justin laced his hands together and set them on the table. He watched as Claire fiddled with her napkin and placed it across her lap.

"You know, I've never asked somebody out so soon after meeting them," he said.

"But I thought I was just showing you around town?" Claire smiled and looked down at the napkin smoothed across her bare knees.

"Well, then I've never asked somebody to show me around town so soon."

"That makes two of us," she said. "I don't show many people around town."

"Can we order some wine?" she asked.

Justin gave her a quick eyebrow raise.

He thinks I'm a drunk, she thought. *He thinks I can't talk to him unless I drink.*

"Of course," he said, and leaned back, gesturing to the waiter. He didn't snap his fingers, didn't speak aloud; he only nodded his head and the waiter came.

Claire appreciated this skill. She had been a waitress for a short time, at a greasy spoon between Farmington and Maize, and she remembered being whistled at, shouted at, even clapped at once by a particularly impatient older woman, her teeth in a small glass cup next to her orange juice.

The waiter poured wine into large, bulbous glasses. Claire thought she might know him from high school.

"Can I get you anything else?" He looked at Claire. If he remembered her, his face didn't contain any trace of that memory.

I shouldn't think myself so famous, she thought. *Not everyone is looking. Not everyone knows me.*

"I find it hard to imagine that you don't get asked out often." Justin spoke down at the laminated menu, then darted his eyes to her.

Claire blushed. "I'm not that easy to get to know," she said. She wondered exactly what she was doing here with this man. Here, at least, was something new, though she wondered what she'd say when he found out, as he inevitably would, about Sam. She decided to set that aside for now.

Claire ordered a salad. When she reached for her glass of wine, she watched her hand carefully to make sure that it didn't shake.

"I'm nervous," she said aloud. She tried to swirl the wine in her glass and spilled a red stream down the side of her hand. "It's been such a long time since I've been out on a date."

Justin ordered something heavy, a slab of meat with a side of baked potato—the kind of meal that always made Claire feel as though she had eaten a brick afterward.

"I haven't really been on a date in a long time either," he said. "I just ended a three-year relationship. I guess you can't really call that dating."

Oh Jesus, she thought, but only smiled.

"Well, I guess we're both out of practice," she said.

He began to speak, in response to a question she'd asked about where he had grown up. She was surprised at how much he could talk, once prompted. He told her about his family, how he had lived in poverty at the edge of a small, muddy town in Upstate New York.

"That's what I remember most," he said. "All that mud. After the snow melted, after the rains in the autumn and in the spring. I remember losing a pair of shoes in that mud on my way to the school bus."

Claire told him that she had grown up in Farmington, that she and her brother had gone to school at Farmington Elementary, Farmington Middle School, and Farmington High. That she had spent her teenage years standing around in front of the Farmington strip mall with its two-screen movie theatre, wearing bright, tacky lip gloss, hoping that some boy from the high school would see her and ask her to go riding around town with him or even pay for a movie ticket. She didn't tell him that when she was fourteen, usually her brother was there too, and that she was just as happy when he took her to a movie as she would have been with some strange boy.

"Does your brother still live in town?"

Justin poured her a new glass each time hers ran out.

"Yes," she said. "He's still here." That was true, at least.

Justin nodded. He didn't ask anything further and she didn't say anything more.

Claire imagined Sam crouched in the far left corner of the restaurant, behind the enormous ficus. She imagined him throwing her a glare and scuttling away, through the front door, out into the darkness of Farmington.

I am right here, in this restaurant, she assured herself. *I'm not anywhere else. And Sam isn't here. He's in the graveyard, only bones and clothes.* And as soon as she thought of it, she felt him again, his hands on her shoulders. She closed her eyes, shook her head, opened them again, and listened carefully to Justin, avoiding anything darting in the corner of her eye. Soon, she was able to focus on Justin's words.

After they had finished their dinner and their wine, after the tea candle in its little crystal cup had burned down to just liquid, she asked him to tell her more about himself. She saw him blurry through the dim lights. The waiter came and went, almost silently.

He told her about his ex-girlfriend Karen. He spoke fondly of her, which Claire liked.

"We didn't share the same idea of what life should be about," he said.

"What do you think life should be about?" she asked.

Claire watched as he thought. He couldn't hide anything; everything he thought passed across his face like a hand through water.

"It should be about doing something of value for as many people as possible," he said. He nodded. "Yes. That's it. You could do that in lots of professions—working at a liquor store, as an accountant, anything that involves helping people get what they want or need."

She laughed. "Even as a librarian? I mean, I understand how a liquor store does something of value, but surely not a librarian!" She was joking, but he didn't seem to know it.

"Yes!" he said. "Librarians do a great service!"

Claire laughed. She saw her old history teacher looking at them, smiling under his grey beard. She looked down at the plate at the food she hadn't eaten. She didn't want people from her past looking at her.

Justin told her that he loved Farmington and had since the first time he saw it. "I wanted to live here, he said, to be a part of it. I've never felt like that before. I wanted to help. I wanted to give it something. This company is all I have. So that's what I'm here to give."

"All those factories, empty, flooded and rain damaged, the floors broken." He shook his head. "I had to do something."

"So you want to improve us," she said. "Are we so backward?"

Justin's face had grown red and hectic. He raised a hand, knocking over the salt shaker.

"No, I don't mean that. This is a beautiful town; it has so much—"

Claire laughed and clicked her teeth against her wine glass. She couldn't remember how much she had drunk. She couldn't quite remember if they had ordered another bottle. "I was kidding," she said. "I was only kidding."

"It's important that I don't think that way—that I'm here to fix you." He held up his fingers, air-quoting the word *fix*.

Claire giggled and sipped her wine. "Here to renovate us, then," she said.

"It's a question worth asking," he said, sitting back in his chair. He sighed and grew serious, setting down his glass. He fixed his eyes on Claire.

She wondered in that moment how she could have even considered not accompanying him to dinner. When he looked at her, the wine glass, the nondescript watercolour on the wall above her head, he was really seeing her. Here, finally, was somebody that wasn't seeing Sam when he looked at her. He didn't know—he couldn't. That was the trick: to be with somebody who didn't and would never know.

"I don't want to make your town better," he said. "I want to help it to be what it once was. I want to bring it back to that, you know?"

Claire nodded. She didn't know quite what he meant—what exactly had Farmington been? A small manufacturing town, scenic but unremarkable. It could never be a manufacturing town again. But he spoke with such conviction that the content of what he said didn't much matter. For a moment, she, too, believed that a handful of service jobs might make Farmington a better place.

Claire wanted to reach out and touch his hand, but she kept her hands back and waited.

Claire noticed the waiters and waitresses fidgeting around the edges of the restaurant, stacking the menus, arranging chairs so that they were flush against the tables. It must be almost closing time. They were the last customers left.

"I have to go to work in the morning," Claire said.

Justin nodded. "Let me get the cheque and I'll take you home."

She almost invited him inside. She got so far as to open the door, planning to ask him in for a nightcap or a cup of coffee, depending on where he wanted to go or when he had to wake up. But when she opened her mouth, she felt it fill with cold air, like a billow of air from the freezer. Her living room was cold, so cold that she let go of the door and let it shut behind her. Sam was here, waiting for her. She turned to Justin.

"I must have left the air conditioner on," she said. She cupped her hands around her elbows and hugged her arms against her chest. The cold made her teeth ache, she had breathed it so fully.

"Well, I better let you go to sleep," he said. He didn't mention the cold. Perhaps he didn't feel it. She was no longer completely sure if what she felt and experienced was real only to her.

"Thank you for dinner," she said.

"Would you do it again, then?"

"Yes."

Claire walked through the icy kitchen to her bedroom. She threw open the window.

"Sam," she said. "What do you want me to do?"

He didn't speak to her or touch her. The room was warm and damp with night air. She shut the window and crawled into bed.

She dreamed she was in the library. Justin was seated at one of the long wooden tables, an enormous book open before him—a book as large as the unabridged dictionary kept on its own podium on the third floor. In the dream, he was waiting for her to finish work, which consisted of opening each book to make sure that the words were in the right order. When she opened a new book, the words were images, the sentences playing out like film clips. She knew immediately which words had been somehow misplaced. It was her job to rearrange them. She felt a pang at the unfairness of it all, that she should be responsible for what somebody else had done.

"It's going to take me a long time to finish," she told Justin.

He didn't look up. "That's fine," he said. "I've only just started this story."

Justin watched the crew snap and hammer together the shipment of decorative edging, of company-approved rustic-looking wooden tables, stands, and shelves. The coffee shop was almost complete. All they had to do was stock the shelves and set up the coffee machines, which would hum and drip all day. And then people would fill the space with their voices and their bodies, women with their purses scraping up against the counter, men with change and keys clicking in their pockets as they waited in line. Children would pull tea bags and chocolates from the counters, and their mothers or fathers would tsk and put them back. Justin loved these inevitabilities of everyday life. He loved seeing things move in familiar patterns.

He had insisted on taking managerial control of the store for a few months. The idea of somebody else running it had frightened him. He didn't trust anyone else. He didn't trust the factory with a different manager, either. It might not want anybody else in charge. He felt that he had been tested, and he had come out stronger. It had threatened him, had tried to drive him away, but he had not given in. He believed that meant something.

He knew that this was a curious idea, maybe a little crazy, so he didn't repeat it, not even to Claire.

Once, while flipping through television channels, Justin had seen a late night interview with an Australian surfer, a young woman. He'd entered the interview in the middle, as she was discussing paddling to shore after she had fallen from her surfboard, how she wasn't quite sure what had happened to her until she woke up in the hospital.

"And when did you know?" The interviewer leaned forward, her stiff hair reflecting the stage lights, forming something like a halo around her head. Her makeup was garish, lips bright and bluish-red, eye shadow glittering in the harsh light.

The camera panned back to the girl and down her chest, to her legs, revealing that one leg was a stump that stopped just above the knee.

"I knew in the hospital, when I reached down to scratch my leg and there was no leg there. A shark, they told me. I don't remember anything about it."

The girl spoke simply. She almost laughed when she said it, as though the surprise had been humorous, a practical joke from God.

"And you still surf?" The anchorwoman asked, her eyes big and brimming with concern. She leaned forward.

"Of course," the girl said. "Why would I stop? I love it too much."

The factory hadn't taken Justin's leg or any part of his body, but it had made him afraid, and it had tried to drive him away, but still he wanted to be there.

It will be done soon, he thought, *and when it's done, I can begin life again.* He didn't know what he imagined beginning life meant, but he hoped it might have something to do with Claire. It was too soon to say that to her, of course, but he wished it all the same.

He liked the way she listened—she was quiet until she had something to say. There was something sharp around her, like a crackling of static in a cat's fur, but it didn't repel him; she was difficult, like the factory, but not impossible. That night, after their first date, her apartment had exhaled a cold, dry air, like the air in a walk-in freezer.

Still, he wanted to see her again. It wasn't an impossible cold.

IV

I

The fire was not the first thing that had happened in the place where the factory would later stand, that flat piece of land, verdant but not marshy despite its vicinity to the river. Perfect for building.

First it had only been a field abutting the river, its grasses soft and tall. Children who lived near it—who played in the woods, caught snakes, and swam unattended in the river—were afraid to go there. Though the field was inviting, its expanse dotted with wildflowers, covered in whole patches of violets, bluets, or yellow dandelions, the children stayed away. They told stories, said that the grass was so green because there were people buried under it. They claimed a witch had cursed the place—she made it look beautiful so that it would lure people to come and do things they weren't supposed to. Some children had heard their parents talk about *young men and women laying down together* out in the field, about how in the dark couples *necked and petted*.

But mostly it was instinct—something about the grass smelled too sweet, like the candy bricks and windows of the witch's house in *Hansel and Gretel*. Snakes probably coiled in the grass, covered and waiting. The children were suspicious of things that came too easy. They were good New Englanders, like their parents, and understood that any pleasure you got for free was liable to be what killed you.

Their parents encouraged this fear. They warned the children away. Some spun elaborate stories of deaths, of ghosts rising from the river with dripping bedclothes, of creatures that would come and steal your voice, your soul, your heart. The children believed their parents, for the most part, because parents were the holders of all things worth knowing. Some parents used the field by the river as a threat: *If you aren't good, the river witch will get you and bury you in her garden.* The Witch's Garden was the field's name for years.

When the town grew in size, Victoria's Textiles moved in and built their factory by the river, right in the middle of the Witch's Garden. It took weeks to assemble the slate and wood, weeks more to acquire the nails and glass. Local men were hired to construct the building, men who hoped for jobs at this new factory, which would allow them to purchase houses in town, shoes for their children, sugar and cream for pies.

Two young men died in the first month of construction. Two large pieces of slate had slipped from a pulley and killed the men below. The surviving workers went home and told their wives about the men. They didn't want to frighten them, and they didn't mean to burden them, but they could not help it—the stories came from them like sickness and they could not stop it. They told their wives of the blood. One man's head split so they could see the white inside, another had a gash in his shoulder that spurted blood like water from a pump. The man with the shoulder injury was the worse off—the first man had died immediately and they had put a sheet over him, hiding his ruined head, what was left of his surprised face. The second one had died slowly, his blood seeping into the ground that would soon be levelled and patted down to create the factory floor. He had bled for a full twenty minutes before reaching the doctor, and by then he was sweating, speaking gibberish, his eyes rolling to the back of his head. He died that night, his skin hot and red, his lips cracked from shouting.

Following the deaths, construction of the factory was halted for two weeks—long enough for the funerals to pass—before work resumed again with a new crew. There were no more accidents during the construction, at least not serious ones—one man lost the tip of his finger on a saw blade, another twisted his ankle, and another broke a rib, though he didn't know it until he woke up the morning after, his side aching, his lungs and throat raw.

It happens like that, sometimes, how you don't know you've been hurt until it's over, until the injury is so far in the past that you can't pinpoint exactly how it had happened or how you could have prevented it.

II
<hr>

Sam wouldn't let her sleep. It was the only explanation.

Claire lay in bed after work, her eyes closed, the room silent and cool around her. Her blankets smelled of soap and the cat had curled up next to her, purring against her shoulder. But she couldn't sleep.

She wanted to tell somebody what was happening, though she knew she couldn't prove it. They would think she was crazy, that she was just having a bout of insomnia or night terrors and that all she needed was a vacation, a psychiatrist, some temporary anti-anxiety medication at least. Who could she tell, anyway? Justin? Then she'd have to explain that her brother was dead, why he was dead, and why she'd been at the factory that night. Her mother? Delia refused to talk about Sam, for the most part. It would only upset her. Claire wondered how she could live in the same town for over thirty years and still be so alone.

"I haven't slept in three full nights." She spoke to the mirror and laughed. It seemed that she couldn't possibly still be standing, applying makeup to the green and blue under her eyes to hide their colour, to make the vessels under her skin and their secret movement less evident to anyone who happened to look at her. She carefully slid the mascara wand up from the base to the ends of her lashes, trying hard not to smudge the wand across her skin. If she did that, then she'd have to get out the greasy bottle of makeup remover and rub and rub away the colour. She had already done this twice; her left cheek was raw from scrubbing.

She had a date with Justin. It was funny to think of the word *date* at her age. Her other relationships had moved quickly from a few dates to *seeing each other*, to *living together*, and finally to *no longer together*. It was because she'd always vaguely known the men she dated—they were co-workers, men she'd known in high school. She had rarely experienced this giddiness at the fourth date, the fifth date, or, now, the sixth date. He still walked her to her door. They kissed in the wan, bug-speckled glow of her porch light. She had not yet invited him inside. He had not yet asked.

She liked being near him. He was unselfconscious, earnest about everything. When a couple at the restaurant with a small, crying child went outside to calm it, he turned to Claire and said, *I'd like a baby someday*. To Claire, this was a faintly embarrassing revelation, like showing a stranger X-rays of one's own enlarged heart, but he didn't say it with any expectation of response. He wasn't afraid to say what he wanted.

Claire also didn't understand what he saw in the town. How could he like the two-screen theatre with its scratchy, muffled sound and seats so thin you could feel the metal bones of the chair beneath? How did he view the high school, with its crumbling main entrance and the teenagers that slouched and smoked by it after school, their eyes dull and insolent as they stared at the slow traffic? How did he see the new strip mall just outside of town, its concrete whitish-grey and gleaming, the windows proclaiming sales that had been going on for the entire summer?

Claire was both depressed and comforted by these details. Nothing in Farmington would really ever be different. Only the names of stores would change, some trees would be cut down and cleared while others grew in abandoned lots, turning them wild again.

She didn't believe that Farmington could really change. This was the key difference between them—Justin believed that he could exert some force on the town, that he could help *improve it*. Claire had no such illusions. The town chipped away at her, shaping and bending her as the years passed. But she could exert no force on the town. It was itself, and it was not malleable like her, not made of flesh.

She didn't realize that she felt this way until she listened to Justin and his plans and wondered why it had never occurred to her that the town was capable of, or even needed, changing.

Justin spoke about choosing where he was going, steering his company in a specific direction, handling certain *rough waters*. She liked this language. It made her think of him behind the domed glass of a yacht, navigating it safely through black, choppy seas.

Claire applied her brightest lipstick and powdered her skin. She didn't want him to know how tired she was, how she had fallen asleep on a stack of books in the back of the library when she'd gone to repair the torn bindings of an old collection of Dickens novels. She had awakened to the feeling of her own spit cooling around her chin on the back room tabletop. That had been the longest period of rest she'd had in almost two days.

Maybe Sam couldn't get to her in the library. Or maybe he let her have that nap as a tease.

She had reached her limit the night before, as she sat up in bed, crying, listening to the fan clicking above her, the small sounds of her crisp white sheets rustling with her body. So many sounds that she had never noticed before. They were deafening when she wanted to sleep but couldn't.

A few nights before, he'd delivered a hard slap to her cheek. She'd awoken with a stinging jaw, her face blotchy, cheekbone mottled and sore to the touch.

The next night, he pinched her upper arm. She was bruised the following day, two purple quarters on her upper arm separated by a strip of white skin. She had been afraid to fall asleep before, but now she simply couldn't.

She searched the Internet for possible explanations. Parasomnia, for example. She read an article about a woman who woke up with her mouth smeared in blood, gore in her fingernails, her nightgown streaked. Every night, the woman walked to the refrigerator and tore into any meat she could find, pulling apart strings of muscle and stuffing it raw into her mouth. She never woke during this experience, and always only ate raw meat, nothing else. The woman had cured her disease with an intensive combination of therapy and prescription sleeping pills. The woman still twitched and kicked in sleep, but at least she wasn't filling her stomach with raw flesh every night.

She'd also found posts on message boards about poltergeists: people who woke to find their drawers and cabinets emptied, their chairs arranged in strange configurations. They attached grainy cell phone pictures of clothing strewn across the floor, refrigerators emptied onto the tile. It wasn't quite like that, either. What was happening to her was personal.

Then the night came when Claire couldn't fool herself anymore. She felt another slap to her face as she was drifting off to sleep. A pinch to her thigh when she closed her eyes. When she turned over, she felt the blade of a fingernail travel up her back.

Sam had teased her like this when they were children, pinching and slapping, lightly punching her when their parents weren't looking. She had not thought often about this part of Sam since his death, this part that was not always so kind.

"Why won't you let me sleep? Are you angry? Did I do something wrong?" Nobody answered.

For years, if you'd asked her what she wanted most, she would have said for Sam to come back. Now, all she could think of was how to make him leave.

Justin met her at her door, as he always did. He reached out for her hand and led her to his car.

"Where are we going this time?" she asked.

She'd let him surprise her on their dates, as it seemed to delight him. He took her to restaurants she had gone to as a child, brought her to *make-out spots* she'd been to as a teenager. Each place was new to him, and so it seemed new to her when she was with him. He even took her to Willow Park, at the top of Farmington's tallest hill, and laid out a blanket. He had made sandwiches—thin, meagre things wrapped in plastic, oozing mayonnaise and mustard. He also brought a pillow and a bottle of wine. She laughed as he searched the picnic basket for the absent corkscrew and then showed him how to push the cork down into the wine with a butter knife.

"You'll find out," he told her. He opened the passenger-side door and she stepped inside, smoothing her skirt under her thighs.

Don't fall asleep, she told herself. She pinched the thin, bluish skin of her wrist. The pain sharpened her thoughts for just a second, one bright flash, before they dimmed again.

"It's nothing too exciting," he said. "Just somewhere we can be alone." He turned to her and smiled.

"That sounds lovely," she said, even as her stomach sank. Her lips and fingers tingled as though the blood had suddenly abandoned her extremities, heading somewhere more urgently needed.

She knew where they were going, though she tried to pretend as though she didn't. The car turned into the factory's parking lot, the new rocks crackling like popcorn under the tires.

Justin stared at the factory, now illuminated with the new glow of a streetlight.

"You said it would be fun to see if there are ghosts," he said. "I figured what better time than at night to see if anything spooky happens?"

Claire nodded. "Ah," she said. "You remembered."

He nodded. "I've made us a dinner, too," he said.

Claire imagined sandwiches wrapped in many layers of plastic wrap, maybe even juice cartons with little straws poking from the top. She hoped he had brought a bottle of wine. She would need it.

It was evidence of how much he loved the factory that he did not see Claire's jaw tighten as she nodded and opened the car door. He didn't notice how she hesitated as she opened the back door and lifted out the picnic basket.

She faced the factory. She remembered this view, in just this level of light, at just about this time of night.

They went inside.

"Just set that down," he said, "and we'll take a tour."

The factory had been completely stocked since she'd been there last. It smelled like coffee beans, chocolate, and fresh paint. The wood-panelled walls were covered in pop culture posters—Jimi Hendrix, *Animal House*, Marilyn Monroe staring blankly into a mirror. They seemed randomly, almost sloppily placed, but she knew now that this wasn't the case. Justin had explained to her that everything in the store was carefully planned at corporate, from the colours of the chairs and tables to the candy placed at checkout and the selection of and placement of posters.

"It's lovely," she said. She spotted a bookshelf full of used books in the back, vintage checkerboards and chessboards, and a tin Chinese checkers container on the squat table between two burnt-orange couches.

"It's amazing how quickly it came together."

Justin nodded. "I'm proud of it. It's the air, you know? Somehow the air here is right."

Claire nodded, though the air felt too warm to her, full of small objects that threatened to become lodged in her throat.

"Can we have some wine?" She cleared her throat and coughed into her balled fist.

"Sounds good." Justin squeezed her hand and let it fall. He rummaged through the picnic basket.

"I remembered the corkscrew this time," he said. "I wanted this to be special."

Claire could not eat—her stomach rioted—so she sipped her wine. She yawned and looked at the cheese, apples slices, and almonds Justin had brought, each in its own little bowl. She listened to him talk about his childhood, though she couldn't remember how they had gotten on the subject. He sipped steadily from a Styrofoam cup full of wine. He was nervous.

"I'm a survivor," he said, and Claire looked at him. She had drifted away for a moment, imagining her bed back home, how much she wished that she could sleep.

"What do you mean? What happened?"

He laughed. "Well, not like a survivor of an accident or a survivor of a plague."

He refilled his glass and took a handful of almonds. He filled her glass, too. She drank without tasting.

"I mean that I got away from that life, you know? I don't live there, and I don't have to. I don't work at the grocery store. I don't lay asphalt for the county. Not that those are bad things, but they were the *only* things, you know? My mother has been a maid for forty years, and she'll probably be one until she dies.

"She changes sheets and cleans toilets. I'm the only person in my family who doesn't do work like that. I escaped."

Justin turned off the lights at the back of the room, over the coffee table and checkout desk, so they were in lower, kinder light. Still, she saw the beginnings of soft wrinkles around his eyes. She wished that she were awake enough to say the kind of thing he might want to hear. He had told her something personal, something he probably didn't tell everyone, and she wanted to let him know that she understood this. But his words percolated slowly through her head—she wasn't sure if she'd caught everything he'd said. She touched his hand instead.

She blinked slowly, her eyes burning. She felt her hands tingle, her blood grow sluggish, her whole body wearing down. As Justin continued to speak, she heard Sam's voice in her head, telling her to run, to get help, not to come down. *Is Sam here?* She asked herself, and had to remind herself that she was an adult, that she was with Justin right now.

The basement door was at the back of the room, open just a crack. Claire had noticed it when Justin first turned on the lights. Now that they were dim, she could still see it, a slice of darker shadow.

Sam.

"I need to visit the ladies room," she said. Justin lay back, his forearm thrown over his eyes, probably feeling the effects of too much wine.

He'll sit up and lead me back there, she thought. *He'll stand up and turn the lights on and I'll have to go to the right room. I won't get to go to the basement and see Sam.*

She shook her head. *I won't see Sam, whatever happens. He's not here.*

Justin didn't rise or even lift his arm. "It's in the back," he said, "right behind those chairs and the table, near the bookshelf. There's a light switch right by the door. Just feel for it."

She didn't turn on the lights. She walked to the basement door and looked back—Justin was still on the blanket. She pushed against the door. It opened without a whine or squeak of its hinges. She put her hand out and grabbed a wooden handrail—it was slick to the touch. Her feet found the top step, and then the next. They were close and narrow. She went down.

Although she had never been in the basement before, it felt like a place she knew. A part of her had been down here before. She had shouted down to Sam and her voice had reached him in the basement. She must have left some of herself here.

She clutched the railing tight—she could feel sleepiness coming over her in waves. The wine, too, made her drowsy, loose-limbed. She placed her feet carefully on each stair, pressing twice against the stone to make sure that she was actually touching the ground. She saw herself sliding on the stone, breaking her ankle. Then she'd be stuck down there until Justin returned. Or maybe she would smash her head on the ground. Her blood would mix with Sam's and she would be there with him, forever, and it would be over.

Stop it. She pinched her wrist again until she couldn't stand the pain, until her fingers ached from the pressure. She rubbed together her fingers—wet. She had pinched so hard she was bleeding.

She reached the basement floor. It gave slightly under her feet, as though it had been covered with linoleum. A weak stream of light came from the basement window—light from the moon. That was the window, the one the light streamed through. She could hear the river. Claire moved toward it. She didn't know, beyond coming down here, what she should do.

The basement air was clear, still smelling faintly of disinfectant. Nothing moved. She closed her eyes, which had grown heavy.

Sam, she thought, squeezing her eyelids together. *Sam, I wanted to see you. And now I'm just going to fall asleep, if you'll let me.*

Claire felt for the wall below the window. She pressed her back against it and slid down. Her skirt pulled away from her back and the bricks caught and scraped her skin, but she was too tired to care. She rested her face on her knees. For the first time in weeks, she fell asleep immediately.

Sam ran toward the factory. Claire followed behind him, but her legs were heavy and she couldn't keep up. The air was quiet and dry, not damp and windy, as it really had been. He turned around, as he always did, before he shoved his body down into the hole. He looked up at her for the last time, his black hair flipping up and away from his forehead. He grinned. He pushed himself down.

As he disappeared, her legs came unstuck. She ran to the basement window.

"I'm coming," she said. "I'm coming through the front door. I'm coming now."

She stood and ran to the factory's entrance. The front door was no longer shut and locked. It swung open easily. She ran into the dark room, dodging table edges, tripping over pieces of wire and machinery. She slammed her calf into the low edge of a table, registering the pain, moving past it. She kept going, feeling a warm trickle of blood as it travelled down her leg, over the bulge of her ankle and into her shoe. She didn't stop to check the bleeding. This was farther than she had ever gone before.

Maybe I'll reach him. She didn't imagine that she could save him. She only imagined that she could speak to him again before he was gone.

I can tell him that I love him. And then, I can ask him to let me sleep.

She reached the back wall and felt around for the knob. She almost tripped down the stairs, her feet travelling faster than her body was prepared for, but she clutched the railing and managed to catch herself before she tumbled down into the darkness. She imagined that if she fell she would wake up. She did not want to lose him now, not when she was so close. When she could let him know that she hadn't forgotten, that he didn't need to hurt her, that she wouldn't ever forget. *I will not wake up.*

Although it shouldn't have been the case, the basement was brighter than the upper room. Blue light streamed through the windows as though spotlights were trained on the glass.

In the light from the open basement window, Claire could see Sam outstretched on a cloth-covered table. He was pinned to it, his body stuck like a butterfly on display, speared through the chest by a blade. Blood poured down the fabric that covered the machine in long, thick trails. Sam's hands, slightly curled, twitched, blood gathering in his palms, spilling down his fingers.

"Sam," Claire said. Her voice echoed like a shout in an empty amphitheatre. "Sam, I'm here. I made it."

A sound came from him, but she couldn't make out any words. His hands twitched. She came closer, though she was afraid of this gore-streaked thing, which she didn't quite believe was her brother, or the memory of her brother, or even a trace of her brother. Still, she didn't want to wake up. She wanted to talk to him again.

She moved closer to the figure, to Sam, to the heavy smell of pennies and dirt, of blood and sweat. She avoided the hand, palm open and dripping blood. She moved close to his face, not far above the place where the blade protruded from his chest.

A splatter of blood like a birthmark crept up his chin and left cheek. His eyes were open.

It was Sam, as he had been when she left him that night—she could smell a faint splash of Stetson cologne, which she'd given him for Christmas. His hair was long, curling up around his ears—he could never get it to lay flat. He blinked. He moved his mouth and a wheeze came out. Blood oozed from between his teeth.

"I'm here," she said. She touched his shoulder, where the blood had not yet soaked. He made a hissing sound between his teeth.

"I'm sorry," she said. "I won't touch you, I'm sorry."

He looked at her. The blood flowing from his nose was now a long, thin stream. He opened his mouth, which was turned slightly toward her, and a mix of blood and spittle honeyed from between his lips.

"Claire," he said, the world sounding like a gargle. He made a sucking noise when he breathed in. He was drowning in blood.

"I'm here," she said.

"Claire," he said. "You have to get me out." The word *out* ended in a sound like car wheels through slush.

She remembered the closest house to the factory, just two blocks away, where the sidewalk erupted in a long rut—where she had almost tripped and fallen that night. She wondered if outside it would be her time or his. No matter—she would get somebody here. It didn't matter how.

"Sam," she said, "I'm going to go right now and call an ambulance. I won't go home. I won't go far. I'm going to get you—"

"No." A string of sticky blood fell from his mouth. He did not blink. "No. It won't work. I'm already gone."

"So what should I do?" The room grew warmer as she waited. Like a sound from a distance, she could vaguely feel the pain from the scratches on her back, but it wasn't enough to wake her.

"I need you to get rid of it." He closed his eyes and turned his head slightly, wincing. His breathing heaved and his face was slick and waxy with sweat.

"I don't understand," she said. "Help me to understand."

"I need you to get rid of it. Make it go away. Make it so nobody can be here. So nobody can work here or die here. Make it so I can leave."

Claire shook her head. "I don't know how—"

"Do it for me," he said.

His face clenched—he was struggling to breathe. He could no longer speak.

I could tell somebody, Claire thought. *I could still save him.*

But he was already slowing, the struggle seeping out of him.

She watched him until his chest no longer moved, his head fell back and hung loose from his neck at an impossible angle. She wanted to lift his head, to take the pressure from his slim neck, though she knew that he could no longer feel it. She touched his hand and his blood, still warm, felt tacky. She lingered, skin to skin, his blood thickening between them.

Claire. Claire.

The voice was in her ear, a hand around each shoulder. She smelled shampoo and the buttery scent of almonds.

"Claire, are you all right?"

She opened her eyes. Justin was crouched in front, staring at her. She struggled to keep her eyes open, to focus on him.

"I'm sorry," she said. "I was just so sleepy."

"Why were you down here? Christ, you could have broken your ankle coming down those stairs in the dark!"

Justin seemed angry in the same way her father had been when she was reckless while riding her bike.

"I got lost," she said. "I thought this was the bathroom."

Claire waited for Justin to point out how little sense this made. She was beginning to feel the first waves of cold that always hit her upon waking. She wanted to be home, in bed, away from here. She held the back of her hand against her mouth and coughed. Justin helped her up and to the stairs as she held back the sickness. She made it upstairs and to the sink in the washroom before throwing up. He held back her hair.

She began to miss him already, even as he stood above her, smoothing her hair.

On the way home, she apologized for ruining their date, for getting lost, for getting sick. He smiled and reached across the car, touched the crown of her head.

"You can't help feeling sick," he said. "I still had a good time."

She laughed. "Really? What was your favourite part—me falling asleep in the basement or me vomiting all over your new bathroom?"

As they drove through the downtown to her apartment, every light in every storefront seemed brighter, crisper. Even people she knew looked unreal to her when she saw them at night. But tonight, everything felt hyper-real, everyone vibrantly alive as they walked to bars or clocked out from the night shift. She felt more real, too, as though everything dark and leaden had been purged from her.

She'd be able to sleep tonight.

"Would you like to come inside?" she asked as Justin leaned in to kiss her on her front porch. "I have wine."

"But you're sick," he said.

"I feel much better now."

He paused, toying with the links of his watch.

"I'll brush my teeth," she said.

Justin laughed. "There's an offer I can't refuse."

That night, for the first time in a long time, Claire slept soundly. Justin did not snore. He stayed curled at the other side of the bed, not a lingerer or a cuddler. Claire liked this. She couldn't stand to be touched in her sleep.

He left shortly after waking, apologizing for having to go. He had to be over at the factory for job interviews. He kissed her on the mouth and smoothed her hair, said that he hoped that she was free on Friday. She smiled and poured coffee for both of them.

"How long will you be at the factory tonight?"

"Just until six or so," he said.

She nodded. "Call me later on and we'll figure it out."

They parted and she watched from her living room window as he got into his car, adjusted his rear view mirror, and put on his seatbelt. He drove by the book, like a person who'd taken notes in drivers ed.

She watched until his car disappeared over the hill. He was gone.

She left the window and went to the bathroom mirror to wipe the makeup from her eyes. The circles under them had lightened. Her skin was pink and clear, not troubled with blue spots or a throbbing vein in her forehead.

"I'll do it," she said into the mirror. "I'll help you escape."

Miriam ate her cereal slowly as she read the newspaper, scanning the Help Wanted column for the posting she knew she would find.

Today, Justin was interviewing people for positions as cashiers and baristas. He had called her when the advertisement first ran in the *Banner*—to "keep her posted," he said—and she told him each time that she was happy to hear from him, that the progress was exciting, that she wanted to be notified of every new development.

She didn't want to hear about any of it, really. She imagined all of the high school and college kids shuffling in, tennis shoes pounding on the boards, their voices echoing. It was like that girl had said—what was her name, Claire. It seemed wrong for people to be there. But it was silly to feel that way, Miriam knew, so she said nothing.

But still, she wished he'd leave her alone. She couldn't say anything that hinted at this, though. She knew that Justin was not somebody to ignore. Farmington, like the rest of the small towns in the country, was still struggling economically. Justin offered at least a dozen new jobs, maybe more, if they expanded hours after the first few weeks. If she didn't treat Justin well, if she didn't listen to every word he said, then she might come across as inattentive, unaware of how important he was. So she had to call him and smile and leave staff meetings early to shake his damp hand. She didn't trust his sheer exuberance. She found all exuberance suspicious, but his, especially, seemed almost tragic, like that of a character in a movie who you knew, right from the beginning, was going to die because he showed everyone a picture of his fiancée back home.

Jennifer, home again for the week, came down to the kitchen in her faux-silk pyjamas. Miriam admired her daughter's body, so lithe, easily manoeuvring into chairs and around the sharp corners of the table. Miriam's ankles and knees clicked; her muscles ached when she slept wrong.

Jennifer didn't yet have an inkling of those strange, inexplicable pains. She folded herself onto one of the tall, narrow stools along the kitchen bar and reached for the box of cereal, holding the edges of the bar as she leaned.

"Good morning, sweetheart."

"Morning. Hey, what was the name of your aunt, the one who died in that fire?"

Miriam turned from the sink, where she'd been scalding coffee sediment from the bottom of her cup. "Why do you ask?"

Jennifer shrugged. She poked at her cereal. "I thought of maybe applying for a barista job at that new coffee shop in the old factory this summer, if it's still around by then. But I didn't know how you would feel about it."

Miriam seated herself across from Jennifer.

"What makes you think I would mind? I was just a child when that happened."

Jennifer shrugged. "I don't know. I always got the impression you didn't like that place."

Miriam felt her cheeks grow hot. She stood up and went back to the sink. "But why would you think such a thing?"

"We don't drive past it. You never talk about this big new building project, even though it's supposed to be bringing in all these new jobs and money. You talked about that rug company for weeks and weeks before it came to town, and it only hired like ten people. I figured you'd be crazy about this. But you don't say anything about it."

"Well, there's a lot going on in town, more than just a new little business. We have to buy sand and salt for winter. We have that taser case—"

Jennifer nodded. "I know, I know."

"That was so long ago," Miriam said. "Tragic, of course, but it's been, what, over fifty years?" The words seemed incredible to Miriam's ears, though she knew it was true. Over fifty years. Long enough for her to go from girl to adult to old woman.

"So you don't mind if I apply?"

"Of course," she said. "You do what you need to do."

Miriam put her cup in the sink, went back to the table, folded the morning's *Farmington Banner,* and picked up her keys.

"Her name was Joan," Miriam said. "My aunt's name was Joan."

"I'll see you later," Miriam said, not turning to acknowledge Jennifer's goodbye. She left so quickly that she forgot her sweater. Autumn was setting in. The trees that towered above the driveway, dappling it with lacey darkness, had, overnight, developed yellow patches. It would be cold soon.

Justin stood in the basement amongst boxes and boxes of supplies—stacked paper cups, cardboard sleeves that fit around the belly of the cup, and stacks of brown paper napkins, along with many boxes of tea and whole-bean coffee.

The basement was cool, damp, and completely still.

He made himself stand in the middle of the room until the cold seeped through his clothes. He remained there until he felt his stomach churning, faintly.

I won't run.

Claire had fallen asleep on the floor, apparently not affected by the room as he was. He could be as strong as her.

He had heard of places with disturbances in their electromagnetic flow, places that triggered hallucinations, that caused migraines and made people vomit. It was a natural reaction, and some people were more sensitive than others. He'd researched the phenomena and imagined that he was just *sensitive* to something about the factory's basement. He had gone so far as to ask the electricians if there was anything wrong with the building's wiring.

The electricians said that everything was in order.

So Justin imagined that it was just something in the ground, something about the spot where the factory had been built, so close to the water. There were places like that—he'd read about them, too, on the Internet. *Places of power,* somebody had said, though he hoped there was a more scientific explanation for it. He had never been much for the paranormal. Life was hard enough as it was without a whole layer of terrifying things beyond his understanding.

He stood in the basement until his stomach heaved, until he had to swallow fast to keep from spitting, from choking. He waited until he felt the cold so deep he imagined that the tips of his fingers might turn blue and flake away. He waited until his legs turned him and took him upstairs, almost without his permission,

As he bent over the gleaming, bleached-clean toilet, waiting for the sickness to pass, for his body to calm and warm again, he thought about tomorrow. Tomorrow he would interview more baristas and cashiers. Tomorrow he would find the perfect people for each spot. Tomorrow he would begin to make this place useful again.

III

———

Claire bought a small can of kerosene and a clean batch of rags after work. She told the man at the hardware store that she had to clean the rust from an old bicycle chain. She remembered, vaguely, her father saying that you could clean rust or sludge with kerosene. She hoped she had remembered correctly. The man at the hardware store did not seem to care about her reasons and simply took her money without looking at her.

She came home and changed into black jeans and a black shirt. Marcus had left a pair of shoes that she kept at the back of the closet, a strange sentimental token. She put them on and laced them tightly. She would have to go by foot—she couldn't risk being seen in her car, with its dull paint job, cracked passenger-side window, and her familiar Kerry/Edwards sticker still hanging in shreds.

She set out after midnight without a flashlight. She knew the streets to the factory well. She knew exactly how to get there within twenty minutes—by cutting through the Danners' backyard and walking down the sidewalk-less Oak Street. The streetlights there were sparse, but it would take her all the way to the factory side of town and she wouldn't have to take the wide sidewalks of Main Street. Though it was late, there might be people out wandering the streets who would recognize her—people she had gone to school with who remembered her name but nothing else about her, only that she was a fixture in Farmington, like the catamount statue and the deer park.

Claire kept her mind on the path, on making it to the factory without being seen. She had an old black purse slung over her shoulder, bulging with her new rags and the can of kerosene. The fluid sloshed as she moved.

She tapped at the windows, all of which were locked, shut tight. The front door was also locked; no hanging metal lock this time but a padlock.

At the bottom of her black purse were a few rocks as big as her fist. She had picked them up along the way, surprised to find so many rocks so particularly suited to her purpose.

She started with the basement window, the one Sam had disappeared down—the one she had leaned over so many times in her dreams. She was surprised at how cleanly and easily the glass broke. It tinkled as it pelted something below. She took out one of the rags and soaked it in kerosene. Then she held the rag away from her face and lit it.

She hadn't had much experience with fire. When the rag lit and blew into her face, singeing her eyebrows, she almost instinctively threw it on the ground and stamped it out. But she remembered what she was there to do and, despite the slight burn on her thumb, the sickly smell of burning hair, she tossed the rag through the broken window. She nicked the side of her hand on the glass. A cut opened, deep and wide. It was bleeding, and it was probably deeper than she knew, but she couldn't stop now. She'd bandage it later. Her thumb throbbed where the flames had merely brushed across her skin. She ignored that, too.

At first, she saw only a small, uninspired light coming from the basement. She worried that the fire had fizzled out on its own, that maybe it had fallen against the damp brick wall and blazed out. She moved toward the window, careful to keep her face away from the jagged edges. A burst of hot air blew back her singed hair and the fire bloomed—it illuminated the space, and for a moment, before the smoke filled the room, before the flames grew too hot and close for her to watch anymore, she could see into the basement—it was filled with cardboard boxes, which had all caught fire and glowed like kindling in a fireplace. Her heart, which had been mercifully quiet, was now beating hard; her mind, previously possessed by a Zen-like stillness, now informed her of all the possible consequences of her actions. She was destroying a building. She could be arrested, probably would be.

I probably will go to prison, she thought, wondering if she could plead insanity, and if she did, exactly what they would do to her. Would she have to spend time in an institution? The idea seemed almost like a relief. Maybe then she could tell somebody about Sam. She wrapped her hand in one of her leftover rags and threw the kerosene can through the basement window—the fire down there was raging now, sending up black billows of smoke.

She felt as though somebody was watching her, somebody curious: these unseen eyes didn't worry her. Maybe it was Sam, happy to see the job done. Maybe it was a witness who could easily identify her. Maybe she would be pursued and caught immediately. It was hard to care. All she felt was relief: she'd done what Sam had asked.

"I love you," she said aloud, "but you can go now."

Claire made her way home the same way she had come, through side streets, down scarcely lit alleyways, until she was back in her little apartment. She took off her smoky clothes and went to the bathroom to assess the damage. Her hand was cut deep and still bleeding. She could have used stitches, but she washed and mended the cut herself, held the edges together with a piece of medical tape. It would have to do.

She went to her room and packed her last bag, her suitcase. The house was bare of her things, her history. She had skipped work that day, complaining of stomach cramps, and stayed home and packed everything of value. She quickly realized that most of what she owned she could stand to lose and brought three carfuls of clothes, books, trinkets, and jewellery she had never worn to the local goodwill. She threw away old letters from lovers she scarcely ever thought of. She even threw away her datebook. In the end, she was left with just three boxes filled with books, clothes, and some cookware.

Claire stood over her suitcase. Her blankets and pillows were rolled up tight in her trunk, pressed against the spare tire and the rusty jack that she hoped she'd never need. Then she stuffed her smoky clothes into the trash barrel behind her neighbour's house and got into her car, started the engine.

I could drive all night, she thought, realizing she wasn't tired, though she thought she should be. Maybe she'd see the sun rise. She hadn't seen a sunrise since she was a child and her allergies would wake her early in the morning. Sam would often rise with her. They would wait for their parents to wake up and watch the sun come up as she sneezed and her eyes watered.

But Sam was gone, and now Justin was gone to her, too, and Claire was by herself, finally. The town fell away from her like unpinned layers of gauze from a healed wound.

IV

When Miriam experienced a bout of insomnia, she went out for a walk. She always felt safe in her neighbourhood, which was lined with streetlights and hedges guarding enormous yards. She sat up in bed and pulled the mini blinds away from the window. The light hurt her eyes. She didn't want to walk around in the brightness of those streetlights tonight. She'd take a drive.

She rose and threw on the clothes she had left by the bed from the day before. Her husband didn't stir—he was used to her nighttime wanderings. As far as she knew, he had never suffered from insomnia. He slept deeply and heavily—had since their wedding night, after he'd taken off her white dress in the dark and they had groped and struggled until he was finished. She thought of that night whenever she saw him sleeping. He was so peaceful, as though he had come a great distance to fall asleep in her bed.

Miriam grabbed her car keys and gently shut the front door.

Driving so late at night made her feel as though she was doing something vaguely illegal. She drove past the lit windows of downtown, noting how strange they looked, empty but bright. The sporting goods store had decorated its windows with mannequins posed like a family about to take their canoe out on the water, the mother and the father watching as they children stood in the canoe, their faces turned toward the adult mannequins. The scene made her nervous tonight, though she'd never noticed it before. Why would the parents have the children get in first?

Miriam parked in the Tastee-Freez parking lot. She walked across the street to the deer park, which was lit with a dozen streetlights and was, thankfully, empty. Teenagers supposedly used it to have sex, sell drugs, or do other nefarious things after dark, though Miriam couldn't imagine anyone choosing to be in the deer park at night for more than a few minutes. She sat on a bench, far from the fence where the deer were penned in a few acres of wildly grassy and wooded land. Local environmentalists had asked the town to do something about the park—the animals were clearly sick and suffering, their fur falling away in patches, skin erupted in sores, and animal control had to drag dead deer out almost every week—but nobody could decide on a course of action. For years, the town had planned to do something, to set the deer free and unfence the wild grass and shrubs and make a real park out of it, but their plans never quite got off the ground. Deer, they'd found, were difficult to transport—most would die from fear before they arrived at their destination. The park ranger from the Green Mountain National Forest suggested that the town allow him and his rangers to come in and shoot the deer and put them out of their misery. That wasn't acceptable to the environmentalists. So the deer remained in their enormous pen, which sometimes emanated a smell like rotten potatoes.

Miriam looked out into the mass of dark grass and shrubs— she heard a sound, something crackling and falling into the soft grass.

It probably wasn't safe there so far past midnight. She wondered then where the few homeless people in Farmington went

at night, where the woman who talked to herself by the catamount statue went when she wasn't having long conversations
with inanimate objects. The closest shelter was an hour away,
across the mountain range, in Brattleboro.

Miriam stood and walked along the sidewalk until Main
Street met Factory Street. She continued, following the sidewalk, less smooth than the others, the streetlights a bit farther
apart, though Beans had illuminated the space right in front of
the factory.

What am I doing here? she asked herself. Before reaching the
lights, she crossed the street to the opposite side, where the lack
of streetlights would make her invisible.

She sat on the sidewalk, in the darkness, and looked to the
dark face of the factory, at that thick, heavy door, at the new
locks—no longer those heavy iron chains. She thought she saw
something dart around the left side of the building, a shade flit-
ting through the dark: a person or a large animal.

Miriam jumped up to her feet. She heard breaking glass. She
couldn't see anything—the lights blinded her, made the shadows behind it that much darker.

I should go, she thought. *I should tell the police.*

More broken glass and then a soft thump. Something flickered then, on the right side of the building—a flashlight.

Instead of stepping forward, instead of calling out as she
knew she should, Miriam backed away from the street, away
from the lights, until she was hugging the hedges that lined the
sidewalk, trying to disappear into them. Her bowels felt weak
and she thought, absurdly, of the stone catamount downtown
and how kids had said it would come to life at night and stalk
the streets for late-night stragglers.

From the darkness at the side of the factory, a figure in
black appeared amongst a tangle of weeds and trees. It was a
woman—her hair streamed out behind her. She ran from the

factory, passing through the streetlights just across from Miriam. Miriam tightened, afraid that the woman had seen her, but the figure was too intent on getting out of the light and away from the factory to notice anyone pressed against the hedge.

The woman glanced over her shoulder as she crossed the street. Her face was suddenly illuminated, caught in the streetlights.

It was the woman Miriam had spoken to a few days earlier, the one whose brother had died in the factory—Claire.

Miriam remained in the darkness for a few moments after Claire passed. She had probably broken a window, spray painted something on the side of the building, done something relatively harmless but costly—something that Justin would want to know about and fix.

Then, the first licks of fire uncurled from the broken basement window, creating a faint, orange light that Miriam immediately recognized.

She thought it might be her mind running away from her, her tired eyes. She moved out of the darkness and into the streetlight, forgetting her desire for anonymity. The light was exactly what it seemed: fire coming from the belly of the factory.

Heat poured from the lone broken window, smoke squeezing out from the tiny cracks in the foundation. Miriam approached the broken window. It spilled fire and she stepped back.

Call somebody, she thought. *Go to a nearby house, tell somebody.*

Miriam stared into the fire.

It twisted in fluctuations of light and darkness. She thought of how she had never seen a painting that represented fire properly. It was always presented as a block of bright colour, maybe with a few variant hues to indicate movement. But fire was full of shadows, constantly twisting and reaching, dark streaks of amber knotting in strands. If you looked closely, the dark lines became bodies, people reaching up to get out, to escape the heat and the brightness.

Miriam blinked and backed away. She kept to the shadows and walked away from the factory, careful not to reveal her face in the streetlights. She remained in shadow as she walked down Factory Street and across the deer park, back to her car. She saw nobody along the way; she imagined that she saw someone's shadow in the window of the Tastee-Freeze, but it was only a cardboard cut-out of an ice cream cone, absurdly shaped like a curvaceous woman.

Miriam drove home, stripped off her clothes, stuffed them down deep in the hamper, and went to bed naked. She was suddenly exhausted.

When the call came—how much later she wasn't sure—she had almost forgotten what she had seen earlier that night.

V

The first to wake were the ones who lived at the edge of town. The small houses and apartments were the first to feel the heat of the blaze. Crystal Ramirez, thirteen, smelled the fire first. She had been awake in her bed at one in the morning, having just gotten to the halfway point in *Jane Eyre*. Jane loved Mr. Rochester, but she couldn't say anything about it. Mr. Rochester, who seemed to be cruel and full of himself, had dressed up as a gypsy (a ruse that Crystal had seen through, and was disappointed that Jane hadn't) and tried to force Jane to reveal her love. He loved her, of course, but wanted her to suffer. It seemed strange to Crystal that he would want somebody he loved to suffer, but she understood already that men were sometimes like this. Women, too.

She lay in bed, thinking of Jane and Mr. Rochester, how in times not so long ago, it was impossible to state exactly what one thought or who one loved. Nowadays, if you liked a guy, you could text him. It seemed almost too easy.

She sat up in bed—she smelled fire. Whenever her mother smelled fire she sniffed at the electrical outlets, pulled the furniture away from the furnace vents, and generally made a big production of things, making everybody get up and help her search for the phantom smell. Crystal went to her window, which was already open, and looked through the mesh. It was too dark. She pushed up the screen to see clearly through the trees.

In the dark, an orange glow illuminated the line of tall, sparse pine trees between her room and the row of factories beyond, those big empty boxes, the windows black or broken, the river cold and clear behind them.

The trees were on fire. Or the things behind the trees. Crystal watched the light expand and contract, breathing just like an animal.

In town, too, people woke, not quite knowing why but feeling suddenly hungry, ill, headaches like tiny hammers in their skulls. They rose from bed, put on their robes, and went to their kitchens where they sat drinking glasses of water or milk, feeling as though they had missed something, or were late for something, or were waiting for something. And then the fire trucks sounded their sirens as they raced through the empty streets, and the townspeople breathed a sigh of relief. Something was about to happen.

The crowd began to gather soon after—people who lived within walking distance came in their slippers, some with their children trailing barefoot. The children felt their feet on the pavement and the grass between their toes, the blades damp and cool. Most of the children would remember this as a night of rare freedom, like the freedom of family picnics where their mothers and fathers drank wine from Styrofoam cups and let the children wander out past their vision and play games they couldn't play in their parents' sight. The fire, too, was like the Fourth of July, with all those colours in the sky, only better because nobody knew when it would end and the adults couldn't control it. It might light up the trees around it, the buildings next to it, it might even run up the street until it reached the houses beyond. It was exciting, the children thought, to be near something that the adults couldn't control. It was like being near a lion or the ocean.

As the townspeople got closer to the fire, as close as they could come without being shouted at by the firemen and police officers, the children gripped their parents' legs, clung to their thin nightclothes. The adults huddled together. The factory would be gone in an hour if the fire kept travelling as it was, and they wanted to watch until it was gone. They felt, still, that something important was happening, something they needed to see.

The fire department soaked the pavement around the building and sprayed their hoses at the outer walls. They weren't interested in saving the building anymore—it was too late. They just didn't want it to spread to the other empty factories and houses.

"It will burn itself out soon," somebody said, and the crowd nodded or sighed.

Some were old enough to remember the first fire, the day the women had rushed out, coughing, and the picture in the paper the day after that showed them kneeling or standing and weeping in the parking lot as flames burst through the windows. The headlines had said *Tragedy at the New England Textiles Factory.* This, though, was not a tragedy.

Some remembered the death of the boy, the one who had fallen through the basement window. They had known him by sight or name, had perhaps gone to school with his mother or father, or had had him over for dinner. They remembered his sister, that sad double, and how she had cried at the funeral and had tried to climb into the coffin to be with him.

VI

Miriam got a call whenever there was a four-alarm fire. Usually, she spoke to the Fire Chief and then went back to bed, or back to business, or back to dinner. However, when she was told the location of the fire that night, she got dressed. At least she could be there for the end. She put on different clothes than the ones she'd stuffed in the hamper—a blouse and skirt. This was an official visit, after all, not just midnight wandering.

When she got to the factory, it was clear that nothing could be saved. The fire could only be contained and kept from spreading. Luckily, the factory itself was somewhat isolated from other buildings, backed by the river, and the ground was damp from a recent rain.

She found Justin easily, despite the crowd that had gathered to see the last moments of the factory. It was a strange crowd, buzzing, curious but not particularly sad. They felt like she did: bewildered but interested. Justin stood as close to the building as was allowed. His hands were shoved into his pockets. He watched the building burn, his face expressionless. Miriam made her way toward him.

"I'm so sorry," she said.

He looked at her—his eyes were red from the smoke, his face flushed from proximity to the fire.

"No, I'm sorry," he said. "That's at least twenty new jobs lost for the town."

His voice was different than usual—flat, drained of all inflection. Miriam wished she hadn't approached him, that she had let him mourn on his own. She imagined that he was in shock, watching as his building burned. But she couldn't leave him now that she'd offered her condolences.

"I want you to know that we appreciated it," she said. "I mean, we appreciate the work you put into it, your good intentions for the town. I know that you wanted so badly—"

"It's all right," he said. "Nothing can be done now." He crossed his arms and held them against his chest. He didn't look at her.

Miriam nodded and returned her gaze to the fire.

"Perhaps you can build again."

He nodded. "We'll find out. I doubt it, but we'll find out."

Miriam nodded and moved away—he didn't want to speak and she felt her presence stifled him. The heat burned her cheek anyway, and she was suddenly very tired and wished that she had stayed in bed. It wasn't hard to pretend that she hadn't been out there earlier, that she didn't know what had happened—she felt that she really didn't know. What she had seen earlier hardly seemed real.

She watched as the fire roared over the slate, the building blackening under the orange flames, until her eyes watered from the smoke and began to feel heavy and irritated.

She watched as the fire climbed the walls of the building. She felt the heat on her skin, noting how the fire itself generated wind, how it moved like a living thing.

Right after Joan's death, Miriam had sometimes imagined (against her will—if she could have stopped it, she would have) what Joan must have felt when the fire started to burn her hair, then her clothes, and then her skin. Miriam would lie in bed imagining she was dressed completely in fire, wondering how it might feel as it ate through her clothes. Would it tickle at first? Would the heat feel comforting before it burned? And how much would it burn? Would it burn the whole time, or would the feeling fade as the skin numbed and the body went into shock? How long would it hurt? She would make herself cry thinking of this, make herself shake and heave in bed just imagining what might have happened to Joan's body.

She couldn't help doing it again, as the building burned. She imagined herself inside the factory, her skin blistering. She had burned her thumb on a hot pan a few days before. Her mind applied the sting of the burn everywhere—she imagined the feeling on every inch of her face, her arms, her scalp.

The firemen emerged from the billowing smoke. The air filled with tiny, papery tufts of char, the brightness of the fire. They pushed the crowd back, their enormous, gloved hands held palms out.

"It's gonna collapse," one of them shouted, "everybody get back."

The crowd moved away as the firemen again soaked the grass and gravel around the factory with their high-pressure hose.

Miriam stepped back, obedient. They had set a safe perimeter, she knew, but fire was unruly and could easily slip beyond the barriers set for it. The new lawn, freshly bought and laid out in squares by Beans, soaked up the water, overflowing, streaming down the street and soaking Miriam's canvas shoes.

Something snapped within the flames—breaking timber. Miriam, at the front of the group, heard a great gasp and shift. The crowd tightened. Miriam stepped back with the others, their bodies now close. She looked behind her—it seemed that the street was filled with people. She didn't know where they had all come from, how they had heard about the fire, or why they had decided, of all things, to get out of bed on a Monday night and watch a building burn down—a building that nobody had worked in for almost a dozen years. But still they watched, some with their hands over their mouths, heads shaking. There was another crack, and then one of the outer walls buckled inward, sending up a flurry of sparks.

Miriam had never before noticed how animal-like fire appeared, how it climbed, how it exhaled and inhaled, growing as it consumed. She'd never been so close to a fire that wasn't contained. It roared and blackened and fed on the building.

An enormous crack like a rifle shot spit from the flames. The crowd stepped back as one. The front wall appeared to waver. The firemen shouted, "Get back, get across the street, clear the area."

Later, Miriam would doubt her memory, imagining that she had exaggerated the quiet that came in that moment, as if she had been so wrapped up in her own head, in her memories, that the scene was hushed only for her. But it had seemed so suddenly still, like they were all waiting to see the building fall, not breathing or speaking for fear of missing the exact moment of collapse.

Miriam felt her hair blow back from a hot blast of wind as the building let out one last exhalation before the front wall tumbled down, hitting the muddy yard with a solid slap. Water hissed against the fire. She saw the firemen motioning them back, rushing to the truck to hose down the burning pieces of timber, the hot, black rocks, broken and brittle on the ground. Sparks like a firecracker spit from the torn hole at the front of the building.

Something's escaping, Miriam thought. Black smoke rose up in columns, reaching up and away from the source. Sparks flew in great gushes out into the black sky and disappeared, wave after wave like the bodies of swimmers shimmering out into the distance. She felt the heat reaching out for her and shrunk back, along with the crowd. Somebody—a stranger—grabbed her elbow, and she grabbed the stranger's in return. They cowered against each other and turned away from the fire.

Miriam blinked against the brightness and held her breath. The world suddenly felt very still. Something had left: she sensed an absence, the loss of a pain that she'd had so long that she had no longer registered it as pain. She looked up and let go of the stranger, who detached and disappeared into the crowd again. Miriam never saw who it was. The building still burned, the sparks flying like hot confetti over them. A spark fell on Miriam's arm like a fleck of cigarette ash. The slight sting made her nostalgic for those days when she stood by the back door of the Crossroads Diner during break and smoked a cigarette, looking out onto the highway, the cars passing by. She was always dropping ashes on her knees and hands when she smoked as a teenager. She'd never gotten the hang of it in a way that looked natural, as though she wasn't just a beginner. That had probably been a large part of her quitting—not looking sexy or cool when she smoked, but like a kid trying to look sexy and cool but simply burning herself. She had been so eager to get away then, had so wished to be a person in one of those cars going somewhere bigger. But here she was, still.

The fire appeared to be dying—though it was still visibly blazing, the life seemed to have burnt out of it. Whatever urgency the crowd had felt was gone. People started to disperse as the firefighters put their attention on the flaming remains of the building's front wall. They had felt it, too, that great exhale.

Miriam turned and made her way back to her car. She'd lost track of Justin. Maybe he had gone home.

Miriam was fully awake now, with no hope of getting back to sleep. She suddenly wished that she were free to get in her car and drive away from this town—north, maybe, until she reached the Canadian border, then up to Quebec City. She could still remember some French—enough to get by. But she was far past the point of running away from what confused or unsettled her: she was no-bullshit Miriam. Running away because a building had burned down was a prime example of bullshit.

I knew what was happening and I didn't tell anyone, she thought. She shook her head. It didn't matter, did it? It was over now. Claire had succeeded in stopping the project in the only way she could. Miriam tried to rouse the desire in herself to tell someone what she had seen, but she couldn't. She'd have to explain too much: why she'd been there in the first place, why she had come back home instead of reporting it. The idea exhausted her.

She couldn't manage to feel sad for anyone but Justin. But he was young. Life would go on.

She reached her car, cold and dark like something abandoned, and got inside. In the dry, pickled air of the car she could smell the fire in her clothes and hair.

Away from the heat of the fire, she felt the chill. Her birthday was coming soon, she remembered, experiencing a familiar feeling of excitement, as though something important might happen on that day. But she was past the age of gifts, of parties full of family members who wanted nothing from her but to see her grow, past even the age of birthdays marking new wisdom—her fiftieth birthday had been one such, an age that carried some measure of respect. At fifty, one could still prove useful to the world. But it was downhill from there.

On her seventh birthday, Miriam had gone to her grandparents' house to blow out the candles on her cake and open presents. Her mother had baked a spice cake with lemon icing—her favourite kind. She had been more excited about the cake than the presents. She hadn't expected much that year—her parents had just had a new baby, and each year it seemed that she got fewer new clothes, fewer toys, and less attention. There just wasn't enough of anything to go around. Miriam recalled her grandmother had worn bright red lipstick that day, which was strange for her, and had left an imprint of her kiss on Miriam's cheek.

Happy Birthday, my beautiful girl, she had said. Her hands, always dry and warm, brushed against Miriam's cheek.

Joan was there, as she always was for birthdays and holidays, though she bickered and smoked and rolled her eyes.

Come here, kid, Joan said, and jerked her head toward the bathroom door. Miriam followed. Her mother and grand-mother were busy laying out plates and napkins, talking or arguing—it was sometimes hard to tell the difference.

"Look." Joan fished a square, velvet box from her purse. Miriam couldn't imagine what might be inside—usually she received only clothes for her birthday.

Joan handed the box to her. "Open it," she said.

Miriam found the thin, almost invisible seam where the edges of the box met. She pried the lid up and it flipped on a hinge. Inside was a blue and white cameo necklace, its chain thin and delicate, the links so small and perfect that Joan was afraid she'd break it if she touched it with her fat, clumsy fingers. The woman on the cameo was bone pale, her profile sharp, precise, nothing wasted. Her hair billowed at the back of her head in a fat, elaborate knot.

Miriam looked at Joan, who smiled and lit a cigarette. She blew smoke from the corner of her mouth, away from Miriam's face. Miriam realized, for the first time, that this was done out of consideration to her and not just as a clever trick.

Joan likes me, she thought. *She really likes me. Maybe she even loves me.*

"Let's put it on you," Joan said. She took the box and pulled the necklace free, winding it around her fingers. Miriam felt Joan's fingernails brush the back of her neck as she swept up her hair and fastened the cool chain around her throat. Joan turned her around and crouched down to eye level. She threw her cigarette into the toilet, where it hissed.

"You look so lovely," she said. "You're getting to be a big girl now. Take care of the necklace."

Miriam nodded and touched the chilly stone surface of the pendent.

Miriam wished that she had the necklace now to hold in her hands. It was gone, though. She had kept it, for a while, but one day she'd intended to wear it and it was simply gone, not in her jewellery box, not on her bedside table, not anywhere.

VII

In the days that followed, Justin moved in a fog, unable to remember what he had been doing moment-to-moment. He had to call the company, of course, and hurry the fire inspectors to clear him of any wrongdoing. It was clearly a case of arson, but the insurance company had to be assured that Justin had nothing to do with the fire.

"Sorry, my friend, but it's company policy," Gary said when Justin protested. At the time, it had seemed unfair, unseemly, cruel even, to make him report his whereabouts before the fire, to make him prove that he hadn't burned down the place he had worked so hard to build. Eventually, the Fire Chief wrote a statement clearing Justin of all wrongdoing.

It was probably some kids, he had said, his slick black moustache curving down into a sympathetic semicircle.

Later, Justin was embarrassed to realize that his grief, his attachment to the place, had been obvious to everyone. People felt sorry for him. He was some kind of tragic figure in Farmington, a man who loved something so much, and so irrationally, that it was bound to be taken from him. Nobody else seemed all that devastated.

To tell you the truth, the Town Manager had told him in private, *I doubt the place would have lasted more than a year. We're not Burlington or even Brattleboro: people here are content to get their coffee at Dunkin' Donuts. But we know how much it meant to you.* This kind of sympathy was almost worse than silence.

Justin stayed in Farmington, though Beans decided not to rebuild—the historical building had been half of the sell. Without the building, there was no reason to rebuild. But Justin stayed. He quit his job with Beans and became the manager of the local sporting goods store. He took a fifteen thousand dollar a year pay cut, but found that it didn't matter—he hadn't known what to do with all of that extra money anyway, and living alone in Farmington was far, far cheaper than living in Albany with Karen had been.

Having less money freed him. He ate at home more often, often a can of soup in a large bowl, soaked saltines covering the surface. He ate in front of the television or in bed, dripping broth onto the cover of his latest library book—a biography of Lincoln, the myths of the Celtic people, and a strange, musty biography about Marie Curie, its pages freckled with the red specks of bedbugs. He drank less often. He took runs around the block to fill some of the time he had now that the factory was gone, that Claire was gone, that he had nothing to worry about besides himself.

He called Karen soon after the fire. He needed to speak to somebody who understood what he had hoped to do. With Claire gone, she was the only person he could talk to.

His life, he realized, had been very small. Only two people knew what he truly wanted.

When he called, her voice was sweeter and higher than he remembered. She spoke softly, as if she understood that he was grieving even before he told her what had happened with the factory.

"I'm so sorry, Justin," she said. He detected genuine emotion in her voice. It was easier for them to be kind to each other when they were separated by distance. They did not offer to visit one another; they didn't offer their homes if either of them happened to be in town. They both seemed to understand that they would not be happy together and should not try again. He did not tell her about Claire. By then, there was no Claire to tell her about.

The day after the fire, Justin had gone to Claire's house. He had knocked on the door, but she didn't answer. He went to the library, but the head librarian said that Claire was on a two-week vacation. Justin felt the blood drain from his face. He smiled even as his stomach turned.

She hadn't said anything to him about a vacation. *Maybe she's going to surprise me with a phone call,* he thought, and propose that he join her on this getaway, but it seemed unlikely. She didn't seem like the kind of person who liked surprises. He went back to her apartment that afternoon and pounded on the door. No answer. He stood on a flowerbed and peeked in through the kitchen windows—there were no dishes on the table, no cups on the sink. He saw no sign of her.

He went back to the library the following day.

"She called and said she wasn't coming back. She didn't even give a two week's notice," her boss said. The woman shook her head.

"She didn't tell me until this morning, on the phone—no explanation, nothing." The woman pursed her lips. "It's not easy for us, either," she said, as though she were already annoyed with Justin's complaints. "We can't just find somebody with that kind of experience. I wish she'd at least come in and talk to me about it."

Justin nodded and left. He didn't go back to her apartment. He was certain then that Claire had burned down the factory. He remembered the day he'd met her, how intently she had been staring at it, and how he had never found out exactly what she had been doing there. It had slipped his mind completely. From the moment he had met her, he had wanted to tell her about himself, to fill her up with his ideas. But he didn't know anything about her, and she hadn't offered much. Had he even given her the chance?

It didn't matter. She was gone now.

He imagined that she must be a particular kind of psychopath. She had taken everything he cared for—herself, included. She had ruined the life that he was planning, the good work he was going to do. And she'd left him nothing—no note, no word, not a hint of what she had planned or why. For weeks, he would wake in the morning and immediately think, *I hate her.*

But he didn't go to the police and report her. A detective had asked him if he suspected anyone in particular. "No," he said. "Nobody in particular." He didn't know why he wanted to protect her, but he did. Each morning, he would think, *This is the day, I'll tell somebody today.* But it never happened. After a while, so much time had passed that it felt too late.

At first he considered leaving Farmington. Everything there reminded him of failure—of everything he had blindly trusted as permanent, or at least secure. But he didn't want to leave. He loved the deer park, the marble catamount, and the fact that when he drove down Main Street he saw faces he recognized from the café, from the bank, from the grocery store. Children played on the sidewalks in packs. He couldn't help it: he wanted to live here. He wanted to pick a child up from the elementary school, a beautiful brick building right by the Farmington monument, and he wanted that child to call this place home.

When he closed his eyes during break at work, or before going to sleep at night, in those moments when his thoughts moved quickly and he could not catch them, he sometimes found himself back in the basement of the factory where he'd found Claire asleep, her body curled, her arms around her knees.

That day he had been far more afraid than he let on. He thought that maybe her heart had stopped, that the factory itself had taken her because he refused to give in, to go away, to do what it wanted—it wanted him to fail, it wanted him to leave, it wanted to tear away the faux-wood panelling and the piles of napkins and the college-dorm posters in cheap, tin frames. *It's taken her,* he'd thought at the time, *because I'm stubborn and I won't admit that I'm afraid.*

But then she had awakened, woozy, but alive, and he had been so relieved and embarrassed by his irrational fears that he shouted at her for falling asleep. He remembered her slight flinch when he raised his voice.

He had been completely ignorant of what she was planning, even then, when they were together in the very place she'd go on to burn down the next day. It seemed impossible to him that a person could keep her intentions so well hidden. *Wouldn't she want to tell me why, at least? Wouldn't she feel ashamed?*

He hadn't felt a signal in his stomach, a churning nervousness. He always believed in hunches; they were one of the seven secrets to success. But he'd had no hunches. Just a dumb, drugged happiness, the thought of which shamed him now. He wished that he had had some inkling—that he could at least say, *I knew, somewhere, deep down, this would happen.* But he couldn't say that at all. His intuition had failed him.

When Beans decided not to rebuild on the factory grounds, the town bought the land. Miriam spearheaded the purchase.

"We'll make it a public park," she announced at a town meeting. "We'll put a gazebo there. We'll have musical events,

Shakespeare in the Park, craft fairs, a Fourth of July picnic." It felt good to make plans, to transform the black wreck of the factory into something new.

The Select Board approved the purchase and Beans sold the property back to the town at a deep discount. The charred remains of the factory were cleared away and new squares of lush lawn were laid on the black, churned dirt.

It was a beautiful spot, overlooking the river at its deepest point. A white fence kept the park from the shallows, kept toddlers from wandering down and drowning—a common worry among local parents, once the plans for the park had been revealed. They scheduled the construction of a white gazebo, four white benches, a cobblestone path from the gazebo to the benches, and a new swing set in a pit of clean pebbles, deep and with enough give for a child to fall without breaking a bone.

It was difficult to believe that a place so beautiful and clean and untouched could have been a mess of rubble just months before.

Miriam named it *Memorial Park*.

Justin survived his first winter in Farmington. He bought snow tires as soon as the first frost came and rubber grippers for the bottom of his shoes, so he could walk on the ice without falling. In Farmington, the sidewalks were often left unsalted. One morning, before purchasing the grippers, he had slipped and split his chin open, requiring five black stitches. At the hospital, he met a nurse, a woman so young he assumed she must be a candy striper (*but do candy stripers still exist?* he wondered). She was an RN, twenty-five years old. She told him that almost everyone in Farmington injured themselves on the ice at some point—broken arms, broken legs, chins and sometimes foreheads cut open. After that, he thought of his scar—a thin, almost unnoticeable line from his lower chin to where his lower lip began—as a badge, something that proved that he could take it, he could live there, that he belonged now and had the whole time.

By spring, he was dating a woman from town—they had met during a Select Board meeting, which Justin attended faithfully, even if they were only going to discuss salt for the roads or approve the purchase of a new dump truck. She was a kindergarten teacher. He noticed her when she stood to make a formal complaint about a proposed emergency siren that would be placed a hundred feet from the elementary school. Afterwards, he congratulated for her articulate and fair-minded position and asked her out to dinner. Three months later, she moved in with him and graded scribbled work sheets on his dining room table. He cooked, as he was better at it and enjoyed it, and she made the coffee in the morning. This was the life he had wanted, he sometimes reminded himself when he thought of what had happened with the factory. His current happiness was well worth anything that might have been lost.

In June, he received a postcard. On the front was a photograph of a castle in Scotland surrounded by green grass, hills, and more hills in the distance. The postmark, though, was from Colorado. There was no return address.

Go to the Catholic Cemetery on Chester Street. Row 4, number 10. Samuel Thomas Martin.

I'm sorry and I wish that I could have seen you happy.

I hope you have found your home.

Claire

VIII

It was difficult for the locals to remember that the factory was gone, even years after that final fire. The building, its immovable grey presence a fixture since childhood, of school trips, stories, and nightmares, was really gone, and in its place was a pretty park, a harmless place with an outdoor water fountain that nobody let their children drink from, a brightly painted merry-go-round, and plastic animals perched atop strong, steel coils.

The townspeople let their children play there, though. The stories they'd learned as children seemed distant—the dead women dragging themselves from the river, the murderers in the basement, the dead boy who'd whisper in your ear if you said his name at 11:30 at night on September 15th because he was lonely and was only allowed to speak at that exact moment. These old monsters couldn't possibly roam this bright, clean, open place. There wasn't any shadow for them to hide in, and the grass was green and fragrant and frequently clipped down to a reasonable length.

The children didn't seem afraid as they ran across the pebbles, slipping on the unsteady surface, or as they climbed to the very top of the domed monkey bars and hung from their knees, allowing their cheeks to brighten and hair to muss as blood rushed to their heads.

There was still the river, of course, which rushed by, deep enough at its most swollen for a grown man to drown in. The park had a tall white fence around its perimeter, and so for the first time, the children were safe even from the river. *Stay in the park*, parents would say. *Don't go outside the fence. Don't go near the water. A little girl your age was playing in the river after the rain and drowned—they never found her body.*

The river became the monster.

There must be a place that's forbidden. It's a necessary black mark on the map, a place where the monsters, the ghosts, the killers of children, the writhing teenagers, and the devil worshippers go. Otherwise they'd be in the town, living in regular houses like everyone else, unrecognizable in their plastic rain boots, with their bags of salt, applying a thin layer to their perfectly normal driveways every winter. They'd be invisible.

EPILOGUE

FARMINGTON

You had lived there for so long that it didn't even seem like a particular place. It was as familiar as your own skin, as the furniture and knickknacks in your grandparents' house, that lighter shaped like a pistol on their mantel, the tapestry depicting Saint Peter at the gates of heaven just above the green and orange couch. You had walked the entire length of the river from the edge of town, where the sidewalked streets ended, to the other, where the sidewalk turned into the shoulder of the highway. You had gone to every Fourth of July fireworks display since you were old enough to remember and had probably attended them even before, swaddled against your mother or father as the sounds exploded around you and rained brightness in the sky that you could not understand.

As far as you were concerned, you would never live there again once you'd escaped. You imagined yourself selling shoes at the Payless down by the factories, serving truck drivers their black coffee and cinnamon rolls at the café, even teaching at the high school, showing up at seven every morning to ease learning down the throats of the unwilling. You had gone to that high school, had kept your head down as you walked the halls, had felt your teachers skip over your stringy hair, your acne, your clothes, your desperate smell of deodorant. The idea of going back there as an adult made you shiver with fear. What if you became the person you had been just by showing up again?

Sure, there were nice things about it—Old Farmington had its grand houses, its mansion with the miniature dollhouse mansion in the backyard, its private college tucked up and away from the town and its general slump of decline, but those things weren't really in Farmington—they stood at the periphery. Inside Farmington, the river cut the town in two; the train tracks, no longer used, were overgrown with weeds. Farmington was dying from the inside out. You knew this, and you didn't want to die with it. What was it that someone had once said? You can't feel guilty for escaping the sinking ship, even if the people you love won't leave. Or even if they can't leave. You had escaped that ship. It was in the long process of sinking.

And so you left, and you were happy. The place you went had culture, not just those once-a-month poetry readings in Farmington, where the entire crowd consisted of people over sixty, but real culture that everyone had a part in—art galleries, poetry groups, belly dancing, pottery. You began to drink socially, not just out of bright cans on the weekends or from the screw-top mouths of sweet wine bottles. You dropped certain words from your vocabulary, like wicked or upstreet. You learned the complicated knots of roads in your city, which café sold the best coffee, which had the best corned beef sandwiches, and which newsstand sold Italian Vogue behind the counter like some convenience stores in your town sold Hustler.

You went home for every major holiday: Christmas, Thanksgiving, sometimes the Fourth of July. Your mother would say that you looked pale and thin. You'd smile and nod and roll your eyes, the expected responses from the child who had left and made a life far away. They expected you to be slightly dismissive, unfamiliar with the important town gossip, absorbed with your phone and your important emails. And so you were as they tried to tell you about Kelly—you remember Kelly from upstreet?—and how her latest boyfriend had bloodied her nose. You'd made a sound with your mouth and thought about Kelly, that distant memory, and felt sorry for her. She hadn't escaped like you had.

During your visit, you'd go to the corner store to buy cranberry sauce for Thanksgiving or real maple syrup for Christmas morning breakfast or hot-dog buns for a cookout and you'd see someone you went to school with—Brian or Derek or Joe, you couldn't remember which—a boy you'd had a crush on who had not noticed that you'd existed beyond occasionally teasing you during gym class, who now worked at the deli counter, slicing ham and turkey with an enormous blade like an elementary-school paper cutter. You paid the cashier and smiled at Derek, Joe, or Brian, pleased that he didn't remember you but that you remembered him.

After many years, though, you began to change. You watched yourself grow soft and lonely in your city, where you had so many friends and acquaintances, where you knew the best theatres, the best places to get drinks on a Saturday night. You began to see people you had known in your previous life, in that time when you had shuffled home from school, your backpack full of library books and drawings and music magazines with pictures and articles that were like dispatches from a life you could not yet access. You thought you saw Jenny Parker crossing the street on your way from work. She had been your best friend in middle school, but in high school she'd drifted away, had moved with a group of girls with boyfriends who walked through the halls in packs, giggling with high-pitched exclamations of disgust or delight. But there she was, on the city sidewalk, as perfect and untouchable as ever. You blinked until your vision cleared and you realized no, it wasn't her, it was only a woman with a similar fall of ash-blonde hair, the same profile with an upturned nose.

And when you were in the park, eating your lunch, you would find yourself thinking of your childhood, that time when you had been so trapped and unhappy, walking the same squares of side-walk, passing the same weeping willows in the Chestertons' yard, waving to Mrs. Chesterton in April when she began her spring rit-ual of obsessively pulling weeds and trimming hedges and planting rows of bright tulips in the space between her lawn and the wall.

Now, as an adult, during your Christmas, summer, and fall visits, you experienced those walks again and discovered some-thing—you enjoyed them now. Even the memory of that particu-lar sadness and boredom had a sweetness.

The smell of the willows, their drooping leaves, and the river, a smell so familiar and inexplicable that it hit you like a dream come back the next day in full force. The river sent its cold air up from the water, the smell of minerals and salt, the slap of cold relief, particularly after a hot, late-spring day spent walking from school to home.

You began to dream about this walk, the expected turn as you exited out the back door of the school and took the unbroken sidewalk to the Chestertons', to the river, up the hill to the park where the octagonal monkey bars glittered viciously in the sun, and you'd imagined as a child how the heat from the metal might make your hands burn and smoke if you grabbed it. Such a vivid imagination! your mother had said, not always as a compliment. Then you'd scale the hill, shifting the weight in your backpack, adjusting the straps, until you reached the summit, where you could see your whole street laid out before you—the houses and their various lawns, trimmed or overgrown, small and enormous, pocked with horseshoe stakes or old swing set pits in the yard.

You began to remember these walks as the only time when you could be quiet in your mind, the times when you had realized who you were, what you loved, where you wanted to put your attention. You remembered the day that you saw what seemed like a bucketful of rose petals travelling down that river, as though some angry lover had torn an expensive bouquet, petal by petal, and thrown it in the water. What a gesture.

And you began to remember the Christmases, sleeping in your old room, the attic floorboards expanding and retracting with the heat. Your mother turning in bed, your father walking from the bedroom to the kitchen, his bare feet slapping against the linoleum (that sound made you feel slightly embarrassed, as though you were seeing him naked or crying).

On spring mornings, when you woke early to the pale sun coming through the blinds, when your blood jumped at the opportunity to be bared, even slightly, to the air. Boys showed up to school in shorts, though they shivered and their hair stood out from their legs like a frightened cat's fur.

I am becoming foolish in my old age, *you thought. When you returned home for winter, you offered to fetch the maple syrup and the flour just for a chance to see Derek or Joe or Brian in the deli department, to see that familiar way that he pushed his hair back from his head, as he did in Math class. Whatever his name, you remembered that motion, his hands through his hair. But he wasn't there.*

Whenever you visited, you wandered the town, went to places you remembered—the record store on Main Street, next to the old bank that had been turned into an art gallery, or the diner next to the high school, where you had ordered milkshakes and hamburgers after school, giddy with your adult participation in commerce. As you walked among the people you might have once known but didn't know anymore, you missed the days that you had spent away, how you had missed the town's renovation, the artists who had been commissioned to paint the windows of the abandoned restaurants and the general store. You looked at the newspaper, at the births and deaths sections, at familiar last names, and thought you recognized the mouths and eyes of some of the infants, though you couldn't be sure.

But when you visited, you also saw that it was impossible to re-enter—your cousin, a hairdresser in town, spoke of people you did not know, the drama of their lives, and you felt names and professions and diseases and misfortunes and births and marriages and divorces streaming above your head. Too much time had passed.

But then you'd go from the house to your car on the day you were scheduled to go home. You would back out of the driveway, go down the street, take the highway out past the Old Town, those enormous Victorian houses that you'd imagined living in as a little girl—how lucky you thought it would be to walk up and down those grand staircases, to sleep in rooms at the top of the house, those sloping ceilings and round porthole windows that looked over the curving streets of Old Town, over the old graveyard and the catamount statue. As you drove past the row of factories and the new, sparkling park, built in a place where you remembered a factory from your childhood, an imposing slate thing that seemed at one point a fixture of the town. As you passed the park you realized that it wasn't even the place you remembered anymore. You didn't miss this place, but you missed the place you had experienced years ago, as a child. Maybe it was the same for everyone, even those who had stayed, always missing a place that no longer existed.

You passed the last few houses and entered the country, a place where towns blurred, disappearing and reappearing again on the other side with new names, new white churches standing in the middle of the town, where all of the roads pointed and crossed.

They are all the same, you thought. And everybody is from one and everybody misses one and everybody wants to get away.

ACKNOWLEDGMENTS

Thank you to everyone who helped make this book possible at
every step, from conception to publication.

Thank you so much to K.D. Lovgren
for your keen editing eye and friendship.

Many thanks to the MacDowell Colony,
where I completed my first draft of this novel.

Thanks, always, to Zach Trent,
who is unconditionally loving and supportive of everything I do.

ABOUT THE AUTHOR

Letitia Trent is a novelist, short story writer, and poet. Her Shirley Jackson Award–nominated short story, "Wilderness," appeared in *The Best Horror of the Year Volume Eight*. Trent is the author of novels *Echo Lake* and *Almost Dark*, and poetry collections *Match Cut*, *The Ghost Comes with Me*, and *The Women in Charge*. Her short stories, poetry, and nonfiction have appeared in the *Daily Beast*, *Sou'Wester*, *Diagram*, *Waxwing*, *Smokelong Quarterly*, and *Hobart*, among other publications. In addition to writing, she works in the mental health field. Trent lives in an Ozark mountain town with her husband, son, two black cats, and a dog named Sally.

INTEGRATED MEDIA